Table of Contents

Take Me (and My Kids) 1

Chapter One........................ 7

Chapter Two........................ 13

Chapter Three 23

Chapter Four 33

Chapter Five 43

Chapter Six 51

Chapter Seven 59

Chapter Eight...67

Chapter Nine..75

Chapter Ten 85

Chapter Eleven..91

Chapter Twelve 101

Chapter Thirteen 109

Chapter Fourteen 119

Chapter Fifteen 127

Chapter Sixteen 133

Chapter Seventeen 143

Chapter Eighteen.. 151

Chapter Nineteen.. 159

Chapter Twenty... 169

Chapter Twenty-One 179

Recent and Upcoming Last Chance Beach Titles....................... 191

For my dear friend, author Vanessa Grant who taught me many things...the most important being the real meaning of friendship. With love.

And for Ted, always.

Take Me (and My Kids)

Take me, take my kids. Simple. Unless the woman of your dreams has the best reason in the world not to.

Single dad Jesse Carmichael met the perfect woman in Last Chance Beach, but when she heard about his three children, she bailed. Hard.

But Jesse has a plan.

Eva Fontaine has stepdaughters in the custody of their grandparents. She's the only mother they remember, and she moved across the country to be near them. Her life is centered on staying in their lives while avoiding handsome, caring Jesse.

Eva refuses to get involved with another single dad. Falling for Jesse means loving his children. She's done that once and her heart can't take another beating if she should lose them, too.

But Jesse has a new plan to help her and desperate Eva's onboard with it. Until his children throw another insurmountable obstacle in their paths.

Now, Jesse has a plan for that, too.

At Last Chance Beach love takes a stand...

Readers have this to say about Take Me (and My Kids)

Heartwarming. "This is an engaging second chance romance, it is lovingly written about loss, finding love, children and the blending of families and what it entails. This is Eva and Jessie's story how they navigate through all this. It was a great read and I recommend this wonderful story." **5 stars** – Amazon review by Lois

Great family story

Bonnie Edwards has written another heartwarming story featuring well-defined characters that come alive. I enjoyed this story very much and highly recommend it.

5 stars – Bestselling author Caroline Clemmons

Heartwarming ... Touching ... Full of Emotion

"Jesse knows if he is to stand a chance to get through all that 'traffic' in Eva's mind, he needs a plan. And watching that plan unfold will be worth turning the pages."

Quote to remember: Eva sniffed. "I'm pathetic. I'm a mom with no kids. I'm a wife with no husband. And I'm in a battle to save my future with the kids I don't have. No man will want to deal with my huge mess." **5 Stars** – Amazon review by Robbob19

Such a sweet, wonderful story! I love the title. There's nothing like a single dad story.

5 Stars! Romance Author Kara O'Neal (BookBub Review)

How They Met: Weeks Ago

"Hey there," a man said from over Eva's shoulder. Eva turned to face the man. "Would you mind if my friend and I join you?" he asked her with a smooth, engaging smile. Tall, dark-haired, and interested. A second man stood just behind the one who'd spoken.

"That depends," Farren replied before Eva could send them on their way. It would be a relief to change the topic from Grady. "What is your purpose in joining us?"

Eva turned back to face her with a frown.

The men flanking Eva smiled widely. In fact, the man who'd spoken looked happy to answer Farren's pointed question.

"Our purpose. Hm...having a drink and some lively conversation with two lovely women?" he said it like he was guessing and hoping Farren and Eva wanted the same thing.

He wore boaters, white shorts, and looked great in a light blue cotton shirt. The other man was dressed similarly except his shirt was navy linen. They were around the same age. Mid-thirties if she had a bet riding on it.

"Let me guess," Farren said. "You're here for some beach time, golf, and whatever else you can find to do in sleepy little Last Chance Beach." Farren smiled gently because tourists wanted to feel welcome and indulged. "Fair enough." She gave Eva a look of approval.

Eva indicated a couple of chairs at another table. "Pull those over and we'll include you in our lively conversation," she said with a look for Farren that promised retribution.

"Archie Jones," the first man said as he took a chair and set it beside Farren. His friend landed in the chair next to Eva with a sigh.

"I'm Jesse Carmichael," the friend said. "Are we interrupting?" He waved at the women's tablets. "This looks like a business meeting."

"You're not interrupting at all. In fact, I'd like to pick your brains, if you don't mind." Farren pulled her tablet toward her to give them more room on the table for drinks. Archie smiled his thanks and waved for the

server. This was perfect. Not only could she discuss her plans with Eva, but she could get a male perspective at the same time.

She'd planned on talking this out with Grady, but so much for being seen in public together. One lunch and done.

Eva watched the men with amusement. But Farren noticed her friend's eye caught on Jesse's more than once. That meant Farren should focus on Archie.

"You want to pick our brains?" Jesse asked Eva. Her gaze snagged on his and pink rose in her cheeks.

Taking note of the obvious attraction, Farren opened her tablet to her profile questionnaire. "Yes, a few questions," she said. "Nothing serious or onerous. You're both single?"

They nodded and smiled.

She opened two files, one for each man. "Have you been married or in a long-term relationship before? Something serious?"

At the question, Archie looked at Jesse. "Not me, yet."

Jesse nodded. "Yes, I was married, but I'm a widower. Two years ago." He blew out a long breath as if he'd carried the burden as far as he wanted to.

The women offered their condolences, but they were cut short by the arrival of the men's drinks.

Eva watched Jesse with deep sympathy in her gaze. After the server retreated, she said, "That must be terrible."

"It's my kids I worry about."

Farren tossed Eva a look that screamed between them. A widower with kids counted as a single dad. She cleared her throat. "How many children?" she asked.

"Three," he responded. "Two girls and a boy."

"If you don't mind me asking, where are they while you're here?" Farren typed quickly.

"I was lucky because my in-laws agreed to take them. They're busy people so this weekend away is a real break." Jesse's face grew curious. "Why?"

"You walked over here to join two women for drinks. Are you looking for a relationship? Or just a good time?" She leaned in and then back when she realized she must look like a hungry baby bird begging for scraps.

He flashed her a strong smile that showed he was down for sharing. "First, it was Archie who led the charge. Second, did you miss the part where I said I have three kids?" He chuckled. "There's no way for me to find a relationship if I wanted to. Who's going to take on another woman's children? One, maybe, but three? They're young and need a lot of time and attention. So, looking for a relationship is not on my agenda."

Jesse flashed Eva a look, but she was gazing at the tabletop and missed it. In fact, Eva seemed to have shriveled into her seat. Her face had gone stony, and Jesse looked accepting when he read her expression.

Whatever spark of interest had been there for Eva had been snuffed out. It was obvious that his having children had made her withdraw. He was likely right. Finding a new relationship would be incredibly difficult for a man like Jesse.

Chapter One

July 4 Last Chance Beach

"But you promised I could see them this weekend." Eva Fontaine clutched her phone so hard she thought the screen might crack. She eased her grip and held her breath. Her dead husband's mother-in-law held all the cards, and she knew it.

"I don't recall promising any such thing," Estelle Morgan responded. "We're taking Sophia and Jillian to visit their uncle and cousins. Their real family." The girls' grandmother never missed a chance to slash Eva's heart open. That organ bled out, down her chest to the ground beside her fun Italian scooter as she stood in her sun-drenched driveway.

Her driveway. Her scooter. Her children. Eva stood outside Rook's Nest Cottage, her new home in Last Chance Beach and wanted to scream.

But of course, she didn't. Grown women in a battle of wits and cunning didn't scream in despair. No. They handled their problems. Like a boss.

Estelle had no idea who she was up against. Yes, the older woman had won a major legal battle, but Eva had brought this fight from one coast to the other and it wasn't over yet. She'd sold her SoCal family home, quit her job, and followed the Morgans and her stepdaughters to the East coast.

Custody. She wanted full custody of her girls and she wouldn't stop working for it. Not ever. Maybe the Morgans had won legally, but morally? They were contemptible.

"They're Sophie and Jilly," she corrected, desperate to keep their names in her heart.

These conversations had been the same since her husband had been killed in a car crash. What had once been a cool but reasonable relationship with his former in-laws had become a series of emotional skirmishes, tactical ambushes, and legal attacks.

Sophie, nine, and Jilly, six, despised visits to their cousins. The boys were emotionally abusive bullies who had reminded the girls constantly that their real mom was gone, and they had to suffer life with a stepmother. Now that their father was gone, too, Eva could only imagine the cruelty the boys dished out.

Estelle gave a long-suffering sigh on her end. "If you're finished interrupting our day..." And the call disappeared. Estelle had hung up on her again. Eva suspected her calls would soon go unanswered.

Numbly she wondered how she'd live every day if Estelle and Bernie cut off contact. Estelle could get a restraining order if Eva showed up at their door. As it was, she'd barely controlled her urges to follow her girls throughout the day to catch glimpses.

Eva had kept busy the last few months with the move here, buying her cottage, and her decision to open a daycare. She'd found a new friend in Farren Parks. She was heading to meet Farren now. Hmm. Maybe it was time to confide in her friend a bit more. She had to do something to ease the pressure she lived with daily. And Farren listened like a true friend, without judgement.

She slipped her phone into her backpack and then stowed the bag on the rack behind her seat. Eva was due at The Landseer Motel for a morning of lifeguarding, a joyful pursuit that kept her mind off her troubles.

Hoping to patch her heart by keeping busy amid a crowd of single parents and happy children, she settled for the short trip. Her cute, zippy Italian ride was all she needed here on the island and the breeze on her face helped dry her tears and blow away the pain she lived with every waking moment.

JESSE CARMICHAEL KISSED his daughters, Raine and Thea, on their foreheads before they dashed, cheering, into his in-laws front hall. Tyler had already bolted past everyone on his way to the kitchen to see what treats his nana had baked. From the sounds coming from the back of the house, chocolate chip cookies were on the menu.

He passed their backpacks to Sal and Tina. "Thanks again." He braced to say what had to be said next. "No thanks necessary, Jesse. We love having them." Tina's eyes sparkled with unshed tears. "I wish we'd had the time when—well—when they were younger and you two could have enjoyed weekends away." When Lynne had been diagnosed, Tina had quit the family tailoring business to help out, and last month, Sal had sold his shop.

Jesse drew the grieving woman into a hug. "You did everything you could, Tina. Never forget that." He released her and stepped back.

Sal stood behind his wife, stoic and solid. "Have a good weekend, Jesse," he said. "Are you off to Last Chance Beach again?"

At his nod, Sal continued. "It's been years since we've been there. Is it just as sleepy?"

"It's grown some. I'll stay at The Sands Resort which brought a lot of change to town." His eyes caught on Tina's, and he drew in a deep breath. "I plan to check out the Singles' Fest events. You remember I mentioned it a few weeks ago. Archie and I offered up opinions and ideas when we bumped into the owner Farren Parks."

"You're ready to date?" Tina looked concerned.

"Good for you, Jesse." Sal nodded.

"I'm not sure if it's good or not," Jesse admitted. "But this is the launch weekend. I plan to check it out and see if it looks like fun for both the kids and the parents. It sounded great, but who knows? If I like what I see and how it works, I'll take the kids sometime." He also had hopes of meeting up with the daycare operator, Eva Fontaine again.

But that was a quiet, small thing buried in the deepest recesses of his mind.

Sal nodded, but Tina's hand moved to her throat. "I'm glad, really," she said softly. "It's time for you, a young man. And the children need a...a mother." She patted under her eyes with her fingertips. "Look at me, so silly. I'm sure if you find someone special, we'll still..." she trailed away, and Jesse's heart contracted at the fear written plainly on her face.

"You'll always be their nana and pops. Nothing or no one will change that." He hugged her again. A moment later she sniffed and nodded, accepting his promise. By the time he stepped back she'd regained control and was smiling, albeit weakly.

"You go. Have a wonderful time and don't worry about the children one bit. We have fun plans for the weekend. It's the Fourth, so we'll see the parade, go to the fair, let them eat hot dogs and cotton candy."

"And we'll take them to the fireworks tonight," Sal added. "Tyler's old enough to stay up past dark."

"He'll love that." Tyler was four and in a rush to be a big boy.

"Tell us about this Singles' Fest when you get home," Tina said. "I looked at the site when you mentioned it." She bit her quivering lip, looking as brave as any grieving mother could when her son-in-law was open to meeting new women who could impact their grandchildren.

He'd mentioned the dating site a couple of weeks back to plant the seed, certain Tina would investigate. She'd feel more comfortable knowing where he was and how he planned to meet women. Singles' Fest gave single parents ample opportunity to make connections with good, decent people who were serious about finding a special someone. If Tina had hated what she'd seen online, she'd say so. He took her comment as her blessing, hard as it must be for her to think about.

His wife Lynne, their daughter, had been gone for two years and in that time, he hadn't mentioned dating until now. He'd needed to adjust to living and parenting alone. But it was time he opened up to the possibility of a new relationship. Singles' Fest sounded perfect for a man like him.

He gave his in-laws a wave goodbye and turned his attention to the drive and the woman he hoped to spend time with. Eva Fontaine had appealed to him on sight.

They'd met at the bar in The Sands when he'd taken a weekend away with his best buddy, Archie. It had been a strange meeting as Archie took the lead with two beautiful women seated at a table with laptops open between them. He'd told Archie they were likely talking business, but Archie set his hook anyway and got them invited to sit down.

Picking up women in bars had never been Jesse's thing, but he felt like he'd hit a jackpot with Eva. She was gorgeous and smart and had shared glances with him. For the first time since his wife had passed, he'd felt a stir of feelings he'd welcomed.

Everything seemed right. That is, until he mentioned he had kids. She'd grown distant, and any normal man would accept that she wasn't into children. Fair enough. He'd accepted her silent, but clear, no thanks.

But then, he'd learned she had plans to open a daycare and lifeguarded and was involved in the launch of her friend's business, Singles' Fest, which would be full of children. The business revolved around single parents and their children.

Eva's professional life was all about kids, but she'd shut him down cold at first mention of his children. A woman with two opposite sides made him as curious as the next guy.

And Jesse had always been a curious man.

Chapter Two

L andseer Motel - noon
"We had the most romantic meal ever," Farren told Eva as she prepared for her stint poolside. They were in Farren's room at the motel and her friend was reading her to-do-list while she talked about the previous evening. "Grady arranged a table for two on the beach. He'd ordered a perfect meal from The Captain's Table." Eva had eaten there once in the six months she'd lived in Last Chance Beach. It was elegant and pricey, but the meals were divine.

Eva made the appropriate thrilled noises about her friend's impromptu date.

"I'm sure the evening continued back at his place. After all, he's been away for a month." Her expression invited details, but Farren was distracted by what she had to do for the arriving families. Yesterday they'd offered grilled hot dogs and burgers in the center court as people settled into their rooms. The children had flooded the playground and pool while their parents mingled. It had been a great start to the weekend.

"We've got a full motel and still more families have booked in The Sands Resort." Farren eyed Eva and tapped her chin with the tip of her finger. "Remember when we met Jesse and Archie? I thought there was some interest between you and Jesse." She raised her eyebrows. "He's a single dad, right?"

The whole point of Singles' Fest was to give single parents a chance to meet others in a relaxed, friendly atmosphere with planned family outings and for more adult events, babysitting. Eva was a big part of the plan, and she loved the work. It kept her busy and focused while she also worked on the launch of her daycare, *NanaBanana*. Sometimes the pace got to her, but an exhausted woman slept better and had fewer nightmares. At least, that's what she told herself.

"Right. There's no way on Earth I'll get involved with another single dad." She nibbled her lip and shrugged off her doubts about oversharing. "I need to vent; do you have time to listen?"

"Of course." Farren sat on the edge of her bed, hands folded, knees together. "Tell me."

"I spoke to Estelle before I came in. She's taking the girls to their aunt and uncle's place today. She told me last week that I'd be allowed to see them over the weekend and now she's denying me access. She's keeping them away from me."

"Oh, Eva. I had no idea. You've never mentioned this before. I assumed you saw them regularly."

"I kept hoping that soon, I would see them more. But the Morgans have full custody and can banish me if they want." Eva leaned against the dresser at her back. "When I married Rhys, he was much like Jesse Carmichael; kind, loving and sweet. But I see now that Rhys hated confrontation and whenever I asked about me adopting the girls, he'd put me off. He'd change the subject or make jokes about the odds against the girls losing both parents while they're still minors."

"And then the unthinkable happened." Farren's eyes filled with compassion.

She nodded. "I was never told that Rhys had given them full custody in the event of his death. He'd signed the agreement only weeks after his wife had passed."

"They took advantage of a grief-stricken man at his most vulnerable." She clicked her tongue in surprise.

"Maybe, but the fact he refused to deal with it when I asked him to put me in this position now." She allowed a faded smile. "So, would I be interested in Jesse Carmichael and his children? *No way.* Not ever. Won't happen." But, if she were honest, Jesse on his own held some appeal.

She'd be a fool to look for more with a man like Jesse, who clearly loved his children and was a thoughtful, caring parent. She tried to silence her mind but only half succeeded. She'd fallen for a man just like Jesse. Hers had been a wholehearted love; for Rhys and Sophie and Jilly. She'd gone into her marriage unfettered by concern for a future without Rhys. And now, she'd lost them all.

"Thanks for listening, Farren. There's more, but I need to focus on the day ahead of us and you do, too." Her new friend couldn't help as much as she might want to. She wasn't sure how long she could pick up the pieces. "Venting helped."

Giving her friend a wan smile, Eva picked up her towel and water bottle. Farren and Grady seemed to have started something serious and Eva couldn't be more pleased for her friend.

"See you later," she said, and opened the door to leave. "I've got extra sitters ready to come at a moment's notice if any more of the clients want adult time. Emails started arriving last night after people met around the pool." Later today, they planned to herd the group to see the local Fourth of July parade. But first, the pool was open, and it was up to Eva to keep everyone safe.

"You're coming to the meet and greet dinner tonight, right?" Farren reminded her of her promise to attend. "We have a seat for you at our table."

"Sure, I'll be there." The plan was for the men to change tables between courses so they could talk to the single women. It was a way to foster friendships and spark interest without pressure.

Later that evening, Eva shared a table with Farren and Grady. Technically she wasn't here to meet people the way the clients were, but with an empty seat at their table, it had become clear the men assumed they were welcome to sit down. After they'd gone through all but the dessert course, Eva considered the night a waste. She could've been working on her daycare's website instead of feigning interest in small talk.

At least two dads blamed the mothers of their children for getting pregnant and their bitterness showed. After having listened to them whine, she figured the other women would have the same reaction to them as she did. *Blech.*

Grady and Farren had done their best to keep the chatter flowing while Eva had become quieter as the event dragged on. In future she'd skip these dinners. She'd only come to help Farren anyway.

With dessert next up, she was relieved to sit back and sink into her morose thoughts. What were Sophie and Jilly doing? How were they coping with their cousins? Worry rolled through her, useless and painful.

She tired quickly of putting on a happy face when her heart was shattered. Groups of people taxed her patience, a new development for her. Normally she was happy to chat with strangers but these days she preferred to stay separate. Maybe it wasn't healthy, but it was all she could manage.

Farren was overjoyed by the response to the menu, the setting, and the way the men moved from table to table with each new course. Friendships were being forged everywhere. It was clear that the women were relaxed and happy with the support of their tablemates and the men were equally easygoing. No need for awkward pick-up lines or wondering if this person or that liked children.

Everyone here had raising children in common. Laughter and chatter rose to the ceiling as these strangers shared stories of family life. The kind of life that Eva had had with Rhys, and their girls. The life she'd never have again.

On that sour note, she was taken by surprise when Jesse Carmichael sat in the recently vacated chair next to her. His scent wafted by her nose with his movement, and she drank it in. One of her favorites, his aftershave smelled of citrus notes and something earthy. Very appealing.

"Hello, Eva. Nice to see you again." His voice rolled over her and she suppressed a shiver of anticipation at the sound. He could spin jazz at a late-night ratio station because his voice was smooth as single malt whiskey. She was tempted to close her eyes and listen as his voice wove its way to her vitals.

"How have you been?" She couldn't help a dismissive nod with no smile, but technically she'd asked a normal question. She gave a mental shrug. *Good enough.*

Grady grinned a guy's welcome to Jesse. His hand shot across the table and Jesse took it with an answering smile.

"Good to see you, Grady. Farren's got a win tonight. Food's great. Company's easy and conversation's flowing." Jesse shot Eva a side-eye which she ignored.

If she stood to leave, it would be rude.

"Agreed," Grady replied. "Farren will be back shortly. She's talking with Jack, the chef. We've got another idea that the group might enjoy. They're discussing a romantic meal on the beach. But, until it's official, mum's the word."

"I'm not staying at The Landseer, and it's unlikely I'll be around the other parents much, so there's no chance I'll spill the beans. Archie isn't a single parent, and we're here together for the weekend. While the family stuff's going on we'll hit the beach and get some fishing in. We're staying in the resort."

"A guys weekend. Sounds good," Grady responded.

"I'm observing Singles Fest at a distance for future reference. If I like what I see, I'll bring my children next time and leave Archie at home."

He'd left his children at home. *Interesting.*

The weekend they'd all met last month Jesse had left his children with their grandparents, she recalled. Instead of flirting and hooking up, the men had been roped into being an impromptu focus group. Grady had happened in and laid claim to Farren immediately. That was when Eva had realized Grady had feelings for her friend. It had been written across his face for anyone to see.

Anyone but Farren. She smiled softly at the memory.

"Are your children with their grandparents again?" she asked Jesse. *Simple curiosity, that's all.*

"You remember." He smiled ruefully. "My wife's parents have them again, yes."

"Do they know you're here checking out Singles' Fest?" Her voice had gone firm without intention. Rhys had hidden their dating from his family in the early days. When they'd got engaged it had been a total shock to Estelle and Bernie. Looking back, she saw it was another difficult conversation Rhys had avoided until she could share the heat. He'd needed back up before he'd told them he was dating again. She hoped Jesse was a more straightforward man.

Hiding the fact he was dating turned out to be typical for Rhys. He avoided situations that could turn emotionally uncomfortable. And because of that, she was paying the price and had lost their children to his former in-laws.

"Yes, Sal and Tina know. I mentioned Singles' Fest when I got home last time, after the five of us met. I don't want to hide that I'm ready to date again. They're part of my life and my kids love them. Single parents come with baggage and Sal and Tina are wonderful grandparents."

She smiled deeply and held his gaze. How could she not? Warmth spread through her at his words. He wasn't like Rhys, hiding from emotional events.

All through dinner she'd replayed her conversation with Estelle, to see where she'd gone wrong. If she could have said something differently, in a kinder tone, less desperately. *Whatever.* Her stomach had wound up tight as a bowstring. But maybe, some of what she was dealing with now had started long before Rhys's death.

She shifted in her seat, feeling an urge she hadn't had in too long. Jesse's scent, his nearness, had woken her and her heart picked up its pace.

Feminine instinct told her why. He'd left his children behind. Had made certain to sit with her when he could've been at any other table talking to any other woman. Was it a sign he wanted to be with her?

All she wanted was to forget her troubles and loss for a while and the way to do that sat next to her, warm and inviting. There was no more to this urge than physical release. No more than a couple of hours of no thinking, all feeling. Her skin rippled in memory and a warm shiver brightened her smile as she brushed her fingers down Jesse's arm.

She put every bit of warmth she still possessed into the look she gave him.

He was hers. For tonight.

Just to help her forget. She craved peace. And Jesse Carmichael might help her forget the pain of losing her children, give her peace, and a night to remember.

Then she'd never have to see him again.

JESSE WAS HAPPY TO see Eva again. Maybe she wasn't ready to meet his kids, but the look in her eyes was pure invitation to spend time alone with her. They could share the weekend, enjoy Last Chance Beach. She could show him around. They could laugh, share meals, get to know each other, and make plans for more visits.

A voice in his heart told him not to rush things. But he was afraid of the other men here, looking for a good woman like Eva. He'd seen her first. Seen her interest, her smarts, the sadness in her gaze.

He recognized the loneliness she lived with because he lived with it, too. He wasn't sure what had brought the darkness for her, but it was something. She was careful with her smiles, and they rarely reached her eyes. But he felt sure he could help because for a brief few moments when they'd first met, she'd let him see her happy self.

The way she looked at him now made him want to see that happiness again. If he could find a way to help her be happier, even for a short while, he'd do it.

He ate his dessert without tasting it though apple pie with ice cream was a favorite. "What better way to celebrate the Fourth than with apple pie?" *Brilliant commentary.* He was embarrassed by it until she smacked her lips at him and moaned lightly.

"I love apple pie," she murmured for his ears only.

"We'll be finished here soon. Care to walk the beach?"

"Love to," she said, and the rest of the world fell away. The feeling was familiar but ancient, an echo from a former life and a long-ago time, when he was young, and life brimmed with happiness. Back then, it had been Jesse and Lynn, forever.

But forever didn't exist for everyone.

Eva was here, smiling into his eyes, and letting him know he didn't have to be alone. Not tonight.

A couple of people rose from their seats in turn and thanked Farren and Eva for the wonderful evening. After a round of applause, the group rose almost as one and made their way to the exit.

Farren and Grady rose together, while Eva made a show of looking under the table for something she'd dropped. The side of her face was tinged pink, and he had the sudden insight that she hadn't planned on doing anything more than go home. His chest warmed because she'd chosen to stay out with him.

Odd to think that a woman as lovely as Eva hadn't been snapped up already, but no one got to their mid-thirties without baggage. Some had more than others and Eva carried her share.

Farren and Grady moved off to shepherd the stragglers out of the restaurant. The fireworks were about to start and Farren didn't want any of the group to miss out. She was proud of this tourist town and its homespun roots even as Last Chance Beach was poised for maximum growth.

He lifted the edge of the tablecloth to peer under the table with her. "Did you find what you lost?"

Eva's head popped back up in a flash. "Yes, I believe I have." The look she gave him seared.

"Good, the beach awaits."

"Let's hit the bar first. I need something a bit stronger than the one small glass of wine I had."

"Sure, I could go for an icy beer. There are some nice craft ones brewed locally."

"We can take them outside and watch the sky. They say the fireworks over the ocean are fantastic. The sky is darker, making them look brighter."

Jesse rose and held out his hand for hers. "Great, I've only ever seen them in Summerville." When she clasped his fingers, he tugged her into his side, and they headed step for step out of the restaurant and into the rest of their night together.

Chapter Three

All Eva wanted was to forget. Her only goal to be swept away on a sea of desire fulfilled. Jesse Carmichael could give her everything she craved. For now. Right now. To that end, she steered him away from The Sandbar and their plan to share a drink and watch pyrotechnics. Instead, she tugged him to the bank of elevators so they could make their own fireworks. The hall was open to both the front and beach side of the hotel.

Night had fallen, and underwater lights gave the pool a beautiful glow that enticed. The first zip and crackle from the fireworks sounded from over the ocean and she remembered. She closed her eyes against the brilliance in the dark sky. She turned into Jesse's body, hiding her face in his broad, warm shoulder.

"This is the Fourth of July," she quipped as if it meant nothing. As if it wasn't the first anniversary of Rhys's death. She felt sick and hated it. Hated herself for letting Rhys down, for losing her beautiful girls. She'd allowed them to be taken from her when all they'd wanted was to be a family. How sick was she that she'd buried the date so deeply that this was the first time she'd thought of it? Not true, of course, but she preferred self-torture.

Sick with grief she felt helpless. She looked up at Jesse, who look bemusedly back at her. He tilted his head in confusion, his eyes softly focused on her. She touched her lips to his in invitation and snuggled closer to his heat. For a moment she liked this man, truly. This lovely man who could help her forget. She needed to be in stasis tomorrow so she could keep up the fight to get Sophie and Jilly back into her life.

"What's happening here, Eva?" Jesse asked, puzzled. He had a right to wonder, she supposed as she let his wonderful scent wrap around her.

She doubted he'd understand. She barely understood her own needs, but she refused to be denied. She needed to forget, and Jesse could make her.

She brightened her smile although it felt brittle and cold.

"We're going to your room." She punched the call button and then again leaned against his solid, inviting frame, different from Rhys's. She let her hand drift down his strong back and slowly went lower. "You don't smell like any other man," she murmured with an appreciative sniff. Behind her the elevator doors chimed and opened. She backed into the space and gave him the best come-hither look she could muster.

He followed, as expected. "My wife had the scent blended for me."

"Your wife had excellent taste," she offered, raising her face for a kiss. His lips descended and she had a hint of what was in store. He'd obviously been well-loved and that, oddly, helped. He'd understand the difference between being with a woman he loved and being with a woman who needed what he could give.

She wouldn't have to explain when she walked out.

The doors slid shut and they were enclosed. Jesse wrapped her in his arms and held her firmly for an open-mouthed kiss that rolled suggestively through her insides. The pieces of her heart rattled where they'd been broken and frozen into shards. The rattling continued, disturbing and urgent. She urged him on using every call woman had given to man.

She didn't want to remember, didn't want to feel regret or grief. She wanted to be numb, to forget. Her heart needed to shut up and leave her be. Leave her to this man's attentions.

Jesse raised his head from their kiss. "Are you sure this is what you want, Eva? I didn't see this coming."

"Neither did I, but you're here and I'm here and this feels right. Right?"

A flash of regret moved across his face and settled in his eyes. "If you say so."

THINGS WEREN'T RIGHT with Eva. She'd left his bed and now his room without a word and he understood the conversation she'd have with herself. Not pretty. He knew because he'd had the same talk with himself three weeks after Lynne had died. He'd been desperate to forget, to not have to face his children's grief. He figured Eva had just done what he'd done, once.

He'd taken comfort from a woman he'd met at the gym. She'd always been flirty and indicated she was available despite how he'd talked about his wife and kids. But when he'd returned to the gym after Lynne's death, he'd wanted oblivion. He couldn't drink himself there because his children needed him sober. He couldn't work himself into the ground because he had school pickup and dinners to make and laundry to do.

The day Hilary walked over to hug him by the elliptical machines and offered a shoulder cry on, he'd taken it all. They'd gone for a drink in a hotel bar and after a couple or three, found their way to a room.

He wasn't proud of those hours with her and had felt terrible for using her for his own purpose.

Karma, he supposed, because now he understood why she'd been hurt the next time he'd seen her on a treadmill. He hadn't been back to the gym since.

He'd been a jerk and a user.

Even though he understood what Eva had really needed, didn't mean he had to accept being used. She was worth more than this. Something tragic sat in her gaze and he determined to find out what it was.

Because despite the dark reason for her to spend the night with him, he was certain there could be more for him and Eva Fontaine. He'd felt a spark when they'd first met, and he wanted to explore the spark and her. He needed to spend more time with her; real time not swallowed up by passion.

Giving up didn't come easily and he was not done yet with Eva.

After breakfast, he strolled the beach to The Landseer Motel beachfront where he found a group of people sunbathing, swimming, and snorkeling. He recognized quite a few from the dinner the night before and they welcomed him happily.

Eva was nowhere in sight, and he decided to stalk his prey quietly by not asking anyone if they'd seen her.

"Most of the kids here seem like good swimmers," he commented to a woman he'd eaten his main course with last night. Mackenzie Fairfield had a daughter in her early teens and was still reeling from her divorce last year. But she was a lovely woman who was here as much for her daughter as herself. "That's your girl out there with the snorkel?"

"That's her. She's making friends and we both needed time away together."

"Next time I come, I'll bring my children. I wasn't sure how this might pan out, so I was cautious about building it up in their eyes." He scanned the water, but still didn't see Eva. "I heard the pool and playground are rad, though."

"Rad?" She said through a chuckle. "Is it sad or bad that I know how old you are from that one word. Because I think it all the time."

He snorted and gave her a nod. "You think it?"

"If I said it aloud, my daughter would disown me. I was a baby when I first heard it." She waggled her brows in exaggeration.

"Me, too," he responded. "A baby." He gave up looking for Eva on the beach. She was probably poolside lifeguarding. "I'll go check out the rest of motel. Maybe next time, I'll book us in there if they have a small suite. I've got three kids so a regular room would be tight."

"They have a couple of rooms with adjoining doors for larger families."

"Thanks I'll check that out." They said their goodbyes and he headed toward the motel with its bright blue roof. A wooden walkway had been repaired in places and there was a new viewing deck on one side. He followed the sound of laughter and children shouting. The playground lay just past a sand dune and was protected by a chain link fence. Beyond, he saw the pool, with more parents and smaller children in the water.

The Landseer Motel, while older, looked well maintained and accurately described on the website for Singles' Fest. It was a lower budget motel with amenities aimed at families. Clean, tidy grounds with fresh paint gleaming in the sun on the play equipment.

Older wooden lounge chairs ringed the pool deck set in twos and threes, but the pads looked mostly new. Generally, the place looked worn but in good repair and if the smiles and happy faces were anything to go by, the motel had years of family fun left to offer.

Raine, Thea, and Tyler would love it here. The girls were good swimmers because Lynne had started them early. Tyler had missed learning as a baby. Between Lynne's treatments and his job, there was never time for swim lessons. But he'd change that now. When he got home, he'd book classes for his son and soon, Tyler'd be safe around water.

Jesse settled his arms along the top of the fence and took in the sight of the happy mayhem. Still, he saw no sign of Eva.

EVA WATCHED AS FARREN went to her dresser for her clothes. They were in Farren's motel room again. It was also a break room for Eva. She'd already slipped a brown bag lunch into the mini fridge. She hoped to keep her mind off Jesse and ignore the sick feeling in her belly because of what she'd done.

She didn't feel guilty for sleeping with him. Not really. Given the pain she was in, he'd been exactly what she needed. But she'd treated him as if he were disposable after they'd slept together, and it was her treatment of him that had put her into guilt mode. It was hard to separate the two things, but that was the bald truth.

Being with Jesse had been wonderful. His gentleness, kindness, and generosity had given her what she'd needed. It was as if he'd known what she craved without being told. In those hours with him he'd ministered to her every desire and kept her thoughts at bay. He allowed her to *feel* rather than think and that had been all important.

But when she'd woken this morning, she hadn't had the courage to say goodbye. Had she been this cold, this calculating and selfish before, and not seen it?

He'd been wonderful while she'd been greedy and callous. *Not a good look, Fontaine.*

"The group for Barnacle Bill's Minigolf is leaving at nine thirty. Tee off starts at ten." Farren spoke brightly, encouraged by the success of last night's dinner. "Have you had many requests for sitters?"

The question pulled Eva back into the here and now and she set aside her self-examination. It was ugly, anyway, and she doubted she'd find a redeeming moment in her behavior.

"My phone blew up overnight," she said in an attempt at normalcy. She'd spent an hour after leaving The Sands matching sitters with families. "Every sitter I've found is booked for tonight. I may need to beat the bushes for more teens for the rest of the summer." But she'd be happy to fill in time offering work to young people.

"Fantastic." Farren took clothes into the bathroom with her and kept the door cracked open so they could talk as she changed.

Eva stripped down to her bathing suit. She pulled off her shorts first while Farren went to fix her hair in the bathroom. Leaving the door open so they could talk, Farren asked, "How was your evening? I lost track of you when Grady and I got outside."

"I didn't actually leave the hotel," Eva admitted. She should probably lie, but Farren wasn't a judgmental type. After all, she was in the matchmaking business. She pulled off her tee and when her face popped out of the material, saw Farren leaning out the bathroom door staring at her.

"Did you stay behind with Jesse?"

"Yes." Eva deadpanned.

"But you don't want to get involved with someone with children. What gives?"

Eva nodded. "I don't want someone with children. But they aren't here. Jesse came without them." She bit her lip. "But I won't see him again. He is definitely a package deal and..." she trailed away, as heat rose in her cheeks.

"And?" Farren coaxed as she stepped out of the bathroom, buttoning her blouse.

"And I don't want to talk about it." Eva spun on her heel and hurried out the door. Stupid reaction but feeling like a lowdown user apparently brought out her inner coward.

Exiting the room was her first mistake. Her second was blurting, "What are you doing here?" to Jesse, who was leaning casually against the pool fence watching the families at play.

He turned at her brusque demand. He slipped his sunglasses to the top of his head as he narrowed his eyes. She wished he hadn't because she saw him run his gaze down her body as he took in her tank suit. Her towel hung from her hand at her side and her hair was up in a ponytail and covered by a ball cap. She'd never felt so exposed in her tank suit. Utilitarian, the suit was built for comfort, not enticement.

Inside she shivered at the memory of how he'd looked at her last night. As if she were the most beautiful woman he'd ever seen. Totally focused, and totally in the moment with her. But now, in the morning sunshine, in front of a pool full of giggling children, she imagined he saw her as cheap, crude, and pitiful. She lifted her chin and repeated her question. "Why did you come here?"

"To talk about last night," he said in a firm tone. The breeze caught the edges of his shirt and blew one side open, exposing his abs. The abs she'd run her tongue across several times. She licked her lips at the memory.

Be still, she told her lady parts.

Oh, why did he have to be so honest? So forthright? She forced her gaze to her flip flops, unable to meet his questioning look. "There's nothing to talk about. It's in the past. It happened. And I've moved on."

"I see," he responded drily. "'It' happened. As if we didn't make 'it' happen. 'It' directed our behavior. Not us? Not our feelings, emotions, desires? Things that normal, healthy, adults have?"

She shifted in discomfort. "I'd like to forget last night and if you were any kind of gentleman, you'd let me." She quit studying her toes and looked straight into his face, which was rapidly coloring. "I suppose I should thank you for the good time." There, if that didn't insult him, nothing would.

"Okay." He put up his hands in surrender. "You forget if you want, but I won't. Not ever. I haven't been with so many women that I'd forget one. Even one who was only looking for a good time." His lips thinned and she got a glimpse of his stern face.

"I'm sure that's true about not so many women. I didn't mean to imply you're a player." Jesse had been married for years. Happily, too, if her impression was correct. She had a sudden concern. "I hope you don't feel guilty about what we did. If it was your first time since..." she trailed off, unwilling to raise the question.

He smiled but the twist of his lips was melancholy as he shook his head. "Not the first time since Lynne died, no. But my first time I had the same reaction you seem to be having. I told myself 'it' happened and I wanted to move on."

He couldn't have surprised her more. "Did you? Move on?"

"I did." Regret chased across his features.

Maybe he'd liked the woman he'd been with. As much as Eva liked him. But she couldn't add a man she liked to her life. Not when she needed to focus on seeing her kids again. Being with them regularly should be her only goal. *Was* her only goal.

"Then you'll understand when I walk through the gate and climb my stand and never look back." Which is exactly what she did. As she stalked away, she kept her back straight and her shoulders square. When she settled on her seat to oversee the pool, Eva hoped she never set eyes on Jesse Carmichael again. Surely, he could take a hint.

Chapter Four

J esse watched Eva stride through the gate to the pool area and climb the stand to take her seat. She expected him to walk away and never look back. Archie would tell him to take the hint and find the next woman. But Jesse was built differently. He knew what he wanted, and Eva was it. He regretted last night, but not because they'd slept together.

He regretted not waking before she left. If he'd woken in time, he could have talked her off this particular emotional ledge. He recognized the ledge, had spent time on it and the introspection had made him feel low as a slug. He couldn't leave things with Eva like this.

Now was not the time for him to move on even if she said it was. Now was the time to come up with a plan to help Eva see the great potential they shared. Potential and hope could move the most stubborn hearts.

Rather than wander away down the beach to lick his wounds, he took a seat on a lounger poolside, crossed his feet at his ankles and smiled at the woman sitting in the lounger next to him. "Mind if I park it here for a bit?"

"You're Jesse, right?"

"That's right." He extended his hand to shake hers. "Did we share a table last night?"

"Just for the appetizers. I'm Cassie and those girls with water wings are mine." She smiled widely at her girls, who looked about five or six. They splashed happily in the shallow end of the pool.

"Twins?"

"You're observant," she said with a grin. "They're fraternal twins, so they look like sisters, but not identical. They grow at different rates;

they have different eye color and skin tone. Hard to see all that when they're soaking wet and splashing around."

They chatted for a bit about parenting girls who wanted to wear princess dresses all day every day until the next big movie came out and they wanted to be dressed like superheroes. It felt good to share his experience and to hear Cassie's.

"I left my two girls and a boy with my in-laws, while I check out the activities before I decide to Singles' Fest is right for them." This was what he'd been telling people, but a part of him understood it was a lie. He'd wanted to have Eva to himself for a weekend so they could get acquainted as adults first. Sleeping with her had not been his plan. His plan had been to talk with her, see her interact with other children—as he was doing now—and get to know her.

"It's nice that you have help with your children given that your wife's...gone." Cassie's eyes filled with the sympathy that comes with the memory that he was widowed. Word traveled through the group quickly and he supposed every woman here knew his circumstances by now.

He nodded. "My parents live in Wisconsin which means they're too far away to pitch in with childcare. Now, I believe my in-laws are afraid that if I meet someone and I get serious, that could affect their relationship with the kids." Tina hadn't said specifically that she was worried, but he'd read between the lines.

Cassie nodded sagely. "I could see that happening. It's a minefield sometimes. Especially when grandparents don't have much say." She sighed and looked around at adults talking with each other the same way they were. "What I love about this Singles' Fest idea is that everyone here has children, so you don't have people hiding them, or pretending they don't have baggage. Or whatever games people play when they start dating." She waggled her brows and leaned in as if to share a big secret. "My mother told me to hide the girls until six months in and I'd hooked him good."

His jaw dropped. "Whoa. Okay. Moms, right?" He'd be furious if a woman lied about having children. Or wanting children. Or liking children. Just because Raine, Thea, and Tyler weren't here didn't mean he'd hidden them. He'd talked about them with everyone.

Cassie shrugged. "Mom wants me happy." She sounded forgiving. "But how happy could I be if I lied to a nice man for six months? And what about his broken trust?" Her headshake was adamant. "A huge waste of time, not to mention I'd look like a first class you-know-what."

"I promise that's not what I had in mind by not bringing my kids." He'd never considered hiding the fact he was a father. "I wasn't certain I wanted to date before I came to Last Chance Beach a few weeks ago."

"And now?" Her eyes lit with interest.

Given the speed that gossip traveled, he spoke carefully. "I'm closer to making the decision. You're right, this is an awesome way to meet people with things in common." Maybe meeting Eva when he had had ruined Singles' Fest for him. But he had to work with what was right in front of him, not what could have been.

Cassie seemed like a good woman, but as he looked at her pretty, open face, it was Eva who stood in his way. He let out a silent sigh.

He gave the woman in his sights a sidelong glance and saw her chatting with a boy, making him smile and giggle. The mother looked on and then picked up the child and held him up for Eva to high five the kid. She loved being around children. She was a natural. What he couldn't fathom was why she didn't want to hear a peep about his.

Cassie tracked his gaze to Eva. "You say you were here a few weeks ago?" At his culpable look, she nodded. "I hope you find exactly the right person, Jesse Carmichael."

"Right back at you, Cassie. Friends?"

"You got it."

EVA SETTLED INTO HER seat after her high five with a three-year-old who'd floated on his back for the first time. His mom was proud of the tike. She scanned the pool for any signs of trouble and the only trouble she saw was Jesse, chatting up a mom on the far side of the pool. She couldn't stop a glare when she caught his eye. She'd tossed him glances since he'd sat down, bold as brass, to hit on another woman in full view of the one he'd slept with last night. *What kind of man does that? A player, that's what kind.*

Cassie. Her name was Cassie. She was friendly, positive, and open to meet a good man.

There Jesse sat, cool and collected and charming the woman whose twins were in the pool. Dressed in his swim trunks, a teal-blue Hawaiian style shirt, and flip flops, Jesse looked good enough to grace the cover of a men's style magazine. Or maybe the cover of a romance novel. When they'd talked, he'd slipped his sunglasses up to his head to allow her to see his eyes. He'd given Cassie the same courtesy.

She couldn't believe that when he'd shown up here claiming that he wanted to talk, he'd looked earnest and caring. She hated that he'd put on a front, and she'd believed him. She should be happy that she'd told him to move on.

Clearly, moving on was what he did best. He'd said exactly that when he'd pretended to be sorry about his first time with a woman after he lost his wife. Also, she thought uncharitably, not bringing his children to Singles' Fest reeked of a man out to score with lonely single moms.

When she'd first met Archie and Jesse, Archie had seemed the most carefree of the two. He'd made it clear he was out for a good time and wasn't looking for anything more serious. But Jesse had seemed real and honest, and she'd been attracted to him. As soon as he'd mentioned them, she'd stepped back. All the way back.

She should have stayed all the way back.

After yesterday's phone call with Estelle, last night had been about a need to forget, to feel nothing for a while. Grief and loss had made her a fool and now she got to watch Jesse put on his caring dad routine for Cassie. She shook her head. *Good riddance.*

Of course, she hadn't told him about the disaster her life had become. He had no idea she was in unending, unendurable pain.

She'd got what she needed last night. Oblivion. When she'd woken in Jesse's bed, she'd scurried out of his room like a scared rabbit. She was not into one-night stands. Sleeping with a man meant something to her and she was shaken by her callous behavior toward him.

But from what she saw now, he was every bit as shallow as she'd been. *Fine.*

Farren came out of her room, called to her, and they chatted about the remainder of the day's activities.

"Have you settled your business with the owner of the building?" Farren asked.

"Finally, yes. *NanaBanana* will open in time for the school year." While there were no schools on the island itself, it was a large employer for people who lived on the mainland. She hoped that a daycare center located near the resorts would be convenient for employees. "It's time to advise potential clients the spaces are ready to be filled."

"Another new business for Last Chance Beach is cause for celebration. Not to mention a daycare is a necessity."

"I hope so. Now I can interview for certified people to hire. The building has room to grow, and in a few months, I expect to expand."

"If you need anything, just ask. I'm here for you."

"Thank you. I watched you launch Singles' Fest, so I'll tap you for suggestions and ideas." She needed a simple website with private access to cameras set up in the rooms. She wanted to give parents the option of checking on their children through the day. When Sophie and Jilly had been in nursery school, she'd checked on them first thing when she got to work, at lunchtime and once more before she started her car to go pick them up. She blinked back the moisture in her eyes. She missed those sweet, happy days.

She couldn't recall a time she asked Rhys to pick them up. Had he even known where the nursery school was? She shrugged away the question. Once they'd married, he'd happily handed off the care of the girls to her and she'd been thrilled to take it on.

If only Estelle and Bernie understood how much she'd taken on from the start, they might see the harm they caused their granddaughters.

But fretting didn't help. Nothing short of getting them back would help.

"I have to round up our group to go to Barnacle Bill's." Farren brought Eva back to the present with the reminder.

"You don't need me, do you? I have things to do."

"No, I'll see you later. Maybe you can have some time with Jesse?" Farren tipped her head in the man's direction.

Eva pinched her lips together. "I doubt that. He's chatting with Cassie."

"But he's looking at you," Farren the traitor said with a grin before turning away. She clapped her hands and gave a call for the parents to collect their children for their outing. A cheer went up and a scramble of dripping children climbed out of the pool and made their way to their rooms to dry off. Farren gave them thirty minutes to assemble in the parking area.

Eva watched as the pool emptied and when every person was out of the pool enclosure, including Jesse, she climbed down from her chair. She pretended not to notice the man who waited for her outside the chain link gate.

She walked around the pool to check for foreign objects in the water, but when she found nothing, she had nowhere else to dawdle. She approached the gate and the man who watched her carefully. He had a glint in his eye she couldn't read.

"Are you going with the group?" Jesse asked, as if her dismissal of him earlier hadn't happened.

"No, I have the rest of the day off." She kept her tone chilly.

"Great! I hope we can hang out together."

She slipped out of the gate, being sure to check the latch closed properly before stepping away. "I have business to tend to. I suggest you catch up to Cassie and her girls."

"Oh, I wasn't here for Cassie. She's nice and all, but we're in the friend zone." His face was open, jovial even.

She blinked at that. "Then why are you here? I told you I'm not interested."

"If your reaction to last night were any different, I'd believe you." He kept a respectful distance away.

Farren's high school friend, Denny, herded two boys ahead of the stroller he pushed. He had the most delightful daughter with bright red curly hair and a huge smile. She giggled and waved bye-bye as they went past toward the parking lot.

Eva waved back, but Jesse squatted and cupped his ears with his hands and puckered his lips. With his hands waving over his ears, he mimed a fish and the little girl squealed in delight.

"I'm surprised you didn't bring your children this weekend," Eva commented, needing the reminder that a man with children was off limits, especially a man who liked them this much.

He rose as the stroller moved on. "I wanted last night with you. The weekend with you." He raised his hands to ward off her indignation. "Not the way we spent it. I didn't expect that. Not that it wasn't wonderful, but you have to admit, it came out of left field."

He was stumbling through another earnest speech, and she should put him out of his misery and throw him a lifeline, but she wanted to see where he was going with this conversation. "Go on."

"I wanted to learn about Eva Fontaine. At The Sandbar when we first met, you backed off when I said I have kids. I'd like to know why."

He tilted his head, curious. "Three's a lot, I know. Still, there was a spark of interest before I mentioned them. I wanted to see if we could create something more from that spark."

"By leaving your children at home." She still felt suspicious after he charmed Cassie. They'd put their heads together, laughed. She'd touched his forearm briefly. But he hadn't touched Cassie back. Eva would've noticed. Maybe it was Cassie who'd been put in the friend zone.

His headshake was full denial. "I left the kids at home because I wanted to give you and me time to just be us together. Also, I wanted to give my in-laws time with them. They feel guilty for not taking them more often when Lynne was alive."

She chewed her lip. Her turn to be curious. "And now?"

"After last night, I see that you're dealing with heavy stuff, and you needed to lose yourself for a while. I happened to be the lucky man." There was no censure in his voice, no judgment.

Still, she bristled at the inference. "You're saying any man would've done?"

He shrugged. "Maybe. I don't know." He blew out a frustrated breath. "When I did exactly the same thing with a woman from my gym, I admit her being warm and friendly had nothing to do with my behavior. She was merely a means to an end. And, if I'm guessing right, that's what I was for you."

She squeezed her eyes shut. Jesse was smarter than she'd given him credit for. Deeply embarrassed, she felt heat scorch her cheeks. Every muscle tightened as he humiliated her. Thankfully, they were totally alone and no one else could overhear their conversation.

"I used you," she confessed, "and I'm not proud of it." She felt wretched and he wasn't supposed to figure it out and be this understanding. This had just gone down as her most embarrassing conversation ever.

"Can we start fresh this weekend?" he asked. "Pretend last night didn't happen?"

"No." She didn't want to see his disappointment, didn't want to feel Rhys lurking behind her heart. "I cannot date a man with children. I will not. Eventually, I'd have to meet yours. There's no point pursuing things between us."

"You sound definite."

She opened her eyes and saw when the truth hit him. She wasn't budging on this. Sad, regretful eyes bored into hers.

Jesse Carmichael, one of the good ones, turned and walked away. He headed toward the beach, presumably to wander back to The Sands.

Chapter Five

"I won't give up on her, Archie," Jesse said when he found his friend beside the pool at The Sands. The resort was gorgeous, but they'd been here before and he barely noticed the setting. He stood beside his friend's lounge, hands on his hips. Archie held a fruity icy drink, his sunglasses hid his eyes, and his scruff of beard showed a few glints of silver.

"Seems like Eva's had her fun and wants to move on. Let her." Archie raised his glasses to rest on top of his head. He squinted against the sun. "I may be a hound, but I accept a no when I hear one. It's not like you to press a woman, or anyone, for that matter."

"Fine, you're right." He wanted to spit because Archie knew him too well. "But there must be something I can do that's not pressure, not stalking, and not arrogant." He grabbed another lounger and pulled it over. Threw himself into it with a hard sigh.

Archie shrugged. "She's shown you that there are parts of you she likes, although I can't imagine why. But it's the package you come with that she has a problem with." He made a show of sipping his drink and tipping his glass in a salute. "Since you plan to keep your kids—I assume you are, right? — then you need to bye-bye the woman. Simple."

"You're right. I can't force her to like my children. I haven't explained to them that I'm interested in dating, let alone have met someone I want to see more of." He hated giving up, giving *in*.

"There must be single or divorced moms at their school. Go look there. Maybe your spawn know a divorced mom. There could be one they already like."

None of them would be Eva, though.

"Sure, I'll look closer to home. When Lynne died, I heard from a ton of the available moms at the school. Too many, too desperate. And they all seemed to be in a hurry at the time. Like I could switch off the grief and replace my wife, my children's mother, with a new one. It doesn't work like that, not for me."

"Yeah, I get it. But time's past. Sure, they came out of the woodwork back then, but now, you have the option to look around some." The grin his friend perpetually wore left Archie's face. "Take your time. Go for coffee here and there, no strings, no expectations. It'll be different when it's your choice."

Archie's advice sounded logical, even easy. He should take it.

But he wouldn't.

ONE WEEK LATER

Eva and Farren walked the perimeter of the room, inspecting the paintjob in the daycare. A mural of birds, bees, blooming flowers, and worms in soil covered one wall, while the wall opposite had been adorned with cartoonish depictions of sofas, chairs, tables, and kitchen appliances. The other two walls were covered with blocks, circles, and triangles of primary colors.

"I'm pleased with how this turned out," Eva said.

"It's gorgeous, bright, and cheerful without being cliché. Not all girls love princesses and not every boy likes trucks."

Off to the side was a small room with a Dutch door. The bottom half would be closed to prevent tiny invaders from drifting in to see the infants in their cribs, while the top half remained open for airflow and easy sight lines for the adults. Naptime should be safe, comfortable, and reasonably quiet. Stacks of receiving blankets and cotton diapers lined a shelf. Parents were expected to send food and diapers every day, but Eva needed extra supplies in case of emergency. Babies had a lot of emergencies from both ends to clean up.

"Have you hired the help you need?" Farren asked.

"Done. I've found two recent grads for the toddlers and two older women to attend to the infants on different days. They don't want full-time hours but want to be around the babies. Win-win." She smiled. "I thought they'd have a calm vibe since they're both mothers themselves. Once they get re-certified for first aid, and my furniture's delivered, I can open the doors." Boxes of toys still needed to be unpacked, but she planned to do that tonight after the welcome barbecue at the motel. It was Thursday and guests would start arriving in a matter of hours.

"I can't believe we're both launching businesses in the same summer," Farren mused. "I hadn't expected to have such high demand immediately, but here we are only one week after opening weekend and Singles' Fest is fully booked again."

"People missed out last week, so they booked as soon as they could, I suppose." She'd wondered if Jesse might turn up again but had resisted asking if he'd booked. He'd accepted her refusal like a gentleman, and she'd barely thought of him through the week. She'd been too busy with *NanaBanana* to give him more than the vaguest consideration when she woke, when she walked or drove or ate meals. She allowed a bit more time to think of him while she waited for sleep, but that was only because the night she'd spent with him was recent and her body still craved what they'd shared. Soon enough, that should fade.

And if it didn't? What then?

"Do you have any repeat clients yet?" *Way to ask without asking about Jesse.* Eva felt clever for a full second.

Farren shook her head. "Not that I've seen, but there's still time. Remember, it isn't easy for working single parents to take time away. Not financially and not workwise. Many work two jobs and their weekends are full."

She nodded. Unlikely then that Jesse would ask his in-laws to have his children for another weekend this close to the last time. Another reason to be glad she hadn't wanted to see more of him. He had responsibilities she understood all too well.

"I hate to ask, but have you had any luck with Estelle?"

Eva gave her head one sharp shake. "She let me video chat with them the other night." She frowned. "No, that's wrong. Estelle wasn't home. It was Bernie who let me. I doubt he'll tell her that we had a those few minutes to see each other's faces onscreen. The girls have grown, and their faces have changed. They don't look so young anymore and..." she trailed off at the memory. Sophie had changed the most, had moved into her middle childhood years from kindergartner.

Farren patted her shoulder, gave it a squeeze. "At least you saw them with your own eyes. That's something."

She blinked. "But I shouldn't have to feel grateful for a few snatched minutes of chatting. They miss me. I could see it. Sophie looked like she wanted to have a good talk." Eva drew in a deep breath. "She and I used to have these great conversations about life, about being a teenager and how different she'd be then. I told her once how we'd always be together, even if...even if...a time came when she yelled at me or maybe hated me for a few minutes."

"That's some serious conversation right there. Prepping her for those times? Good idea."

Eva chuckled. "She promised she'd never be like that. Sophie loved to talk about us having a lifetime together."

"Maybe she remembers losing her mom and enjoyed projecting into the future with you."

"Yes. Likely. But with Estelle in the way, that future may not happen." Eva blinked hard. "See? This is why I can't date a single dad. You get that, right?" Her heart squeezed and rose to her throat. She'd unconsciously brought Jesse into the room.

Farren pulled her into a deep hug. "I get it," she whispered and pulled back to gaze into Eva's face. Vague sadness flickered across Farren's features and settled in Eva's chest.

Eva sniffed. "I'm pathetic. I'm a mom with no kids. I'm a wife with no husband. And I'm in a battle to save my future with the kids I don't have. No man will want to deal with my huge mess."

"Then set dating aside for a year or two. At least until you settle things with Bernie and Estelle. It seems to me that Bernie has a softer heart. Focus on him."

Eva nodded. "But Estelle is fierce and I'm not sure Bernie can stand up to her." It was a lot to ask a man who loved his wife, a wife who still grieved the loss of their daughter, to go against her wishes.

"Don't forget, you've got allies in Sophie and Jilly. Also, and I hate to say it, but time is on your side. How is Estelle's health?"

"No issues that I'm aware of. But they'd never tell me if she had a health scare. They'd assume I'd use it against them." She would if she had to. She narrowed her eyes. "I'll call again next Wednesday at the same time. Maybe it's a regular night out for Estelle. Maybe Bernie and I can work out a chat schedule with the girls."

"Now, you're thinking."

"It's nice to have a plan again instead of reacting all the time." If she could get Bernie's help in small ways, maybe he'd be of more help later. But she'd have to be sure not to ask for too much or she'd spook him. "I'll call Wednesday and if Bernie's alone with the girls, I'll ask for another video chat. That will be a good first step."

"Excellent idea." Farren walked toward the door. "I need to get back to The Landseer to set up the grill for the welcome barbecue. For a meet and greet, it worked great last time, so we'll continue."

"I'll follow shortly. I still have supplies to unpack." Her office cubby needed to be sorted and organized. It was a stretch to call it an office when it was a converted closet, but she'd chosen to use the bulk of the space for children. "Did you say that Grady wanted to oversee the foam floor installation?"

"He does. Once he did some repairs around the motel, he got into a groove with handyman work. He's discovered new depths to his character. At least, that's how he explained it. But I believe he wants to get his business out of his head for a while. Focusing on hammering, painting, and fixing things does that for him."

The relationship between her friend, the always-happy optimist and Grady O'Hare, former grumpy recluse was still new, but anyone could see they were hooked and liked it that way.

After Farren left, Eva set to work on her tiny desk and shelves. Her office supplies were sorted and stored next to the pile of diapers in the nursery room, and satisfied, she left for the motel to lifeguard.

As she rode her scooter along the beach road, she ignored her mind's call to think about Jesse. He was gone and she needed to move forward and focus on the mess that was her life. She needed to think hard about Bernie and everything that Rhys had told her about his father-in-law.

Bernie was the one who'd wanted a dog. Estelle said they were dirty. Bernie had owned a hardware store and was appreciated by his customers. He had a steady clientele and hired bored retired men who brought their handyman experience to the job. The other hires were eager teens who wanted to learn about tools or building.

Bernie had been the one to wipe his daughter's tears and to cuddle his granddaughters as babies. Rhys's first wife had preferred to hand off their babies to Grandpa.

Reassured that Bernie might help her see more of her girls, she pulled in beside the motel office and parked close to the wall. Families were already arriving for their weekend, and she made her way through the family groups, smiling and saying hello.

Once inside the first unit, she changed into her tank suit, scooped her hair up into a ponytail and tugged the gathered hair through the clasp at the back of her cap. She slathered her exposed skin in sunscreen and grabbed her towel, slinging it across her shoulders.

Shouts of children exclaiming about the pool and the playground greeted her when she opened the door. Her timing was perfect. She'd guard for the next couple of hours, and then have the evening to alone.

She closed the door behind her and saw Farren hand off a welcome package to a man with three children. Two girls about seven or eight and boy who looked four or five stood beside him. There was no mistaking the man. She knew the shape of him, the breadth of his shoulders, how he smelled up close, the color of his eyes and the kindness in his heart.

Jesse.

He'd come for Singles' Fest, and he'd brought his children. Two beautiful daughters and curly-mopped boy about four. They were practically twirling with excitement, like the other children. The possibilities for fun were endless for them, she imagined.

She frowned when she pictured Sophie and Jilly at Singles' Fest. They'd squeal in delight to have a weekend full of activities with new friends. They'd have a freedom they lacked living with Estelle, a woman who loved rules.

Of course, rules and boundaries were vital for children, but it was how they were applied that could break a child's spirit.

Eva wanted to run in the opposite direction, but Farren depended on her to keep the pool safe for everyone. She couldn't let Jesse's arrival send her into a tailspin.

She drew in a calming breath, then put one foot in front of the other as she walked woodenly toward the gate to the pool. Making sure to stay behind Jesse so he wouldn't engage her in small talk, she made for the stand beside the pool. If she didn't look his way, he'd surely take the hint that she didn't want to rehash their last conversation.

The one-night stand could not be repeated. Could not.

Chapter Six

J esse saw Eva the instant she stepped out of Unit One, the room set aside for Farren and other employees as a break room. Farren stood across a table laden with brochures, a child's beach bucket filled with candy suckers, and a welcome package.

"Welcome to Singles' Fest, Jesse," Farren said, keeping her gaze on his and a plastic smile on her face. She ignored Eva sneaking around behind him as she entered the pool enclosure.

Fine. He suspected Eva might play it like this. Hard as it might be, he was determined not to approach or talk with her. He had lots of other women to chat with.

Raine held Tyler's hand as Thea squealed and hopped up and down to get a better view of the pool and playground in the center court of the motel. He'd seen it last week, but it looked more exciting through the eyes of his children.

"Daddy, I wanna swim and climb and swing and do monkey bars." He peered into the bucket of suckers while licking his lips. His hand settled on the rim of the bucket. Jesse handed him one orange sucker, his favorite flavor, then allowed the girls to choose their own.

"You will have a ton of fun, Tyler. But let me finish with check in here."

Farren checked off a box on her clipboard. His name and those of his children were on the page. "You're done, Jesse," Farren said with a warm, welcoming lift of her lips. "At five thirty, we'll have a barbecue with hot dogs and hamburgers, including chicken dogs and burgers if you prefer."

"Nuggets," Tyler chanted.

"Hot dogs," Jesse said. "Nuggets don't work on a barbeque."

"Oh, all right," his son said through a long-suffering sigh.

"Since the grill's already fired up, that'll be great," he told Farren. "I'll get the kids into our room, and then we'll hang out here for the evening." He glanced around the center court and noted that he wasn't the only single dad here.

"That's what most people do. It's an easy way to burn off the travel excitement and begin the weekend. The motel clerk told you that you have a cot in your room for Tyler?" She looked down at the boy and the inevitable happened.

She tousled his soft brown curls.

They were almost ringlets and soon, the time would come to get him a haircut. Tina would hate it because he got his curls from Lynne. Tyler was the image of his mother at this age.

"We're good. He'll love the cot," he said to Farren. "I'm looking forward to this weekend. We need some fresh air and fun."

Farren looked past him to the small family that waited behind his. The children turned and gave the woman and her son shy smiles. He nodded at the single woman, who looked as excited as the boy standing beside her.

He put a hand on Thea's shoulder to guide her away from the gate to the pool. "We'll be back out here in less than thirty minutes," he promised her.

She grinned up at him with her gummy smile. Soon, they'd see her permanent teeth break through and his little girl would be moving into big girl territory.

As he ushered them away, he heard a clear low-voiced comment from behind. "That guy's got three kids? That's a busy home." The woman's comment confirmed his suspicions.

Most single moms would not want to add three more children to her life. She'd have to be a superhero and not every woman was superhero material.

Maybe he shouldn't have come. He should reconsider his plan to try dating. Maybe in the next decade, when the girls would be older teens and Tyler old enough to understand.

But those ten years stretched ahead, dry, lonely, and barren of personal joy. He wanted a partner. He'd done two years alone and now that he was out of the fog of initial grief, he was ready to live again.

If Eva truly didn't like his children, what better place to find the right woman than Singles' Fest? But he needed to be certain that his hopes for Eva were useless. That might take a bit of time.

The room he was given was directly across from Eva's lifeguard stand. He felt safer seeing the pool and next to it, the playground. Raine and Thea swam like fish, making him free to focus on Tyler. Lynne had been too sick when Tyler was at the age where the girls first took lessons. Life for the toddler had been very different from his sisters during those years.

Jesse had tried to make up for the things Tyler had missed and these visits to Last Chance Beach would help. Starting with getting him into the pool.

He ushered his herd into the room, leaving the door open to catch the breeze.

"Hi, neighbor."

He turned to find another dad waiting in the open doorway. "Hi, there. I'm Jesse, nice to meet you."

"Denny, I'm here with my three, too. Two boys and this punkin."

They shook hands, grinning.

The punkin was a toddler with red ringlets and a wet, sloppy mouth full of fingers. She giggled and waved her other fist in his direction from her stroller.

"She's a beauty."

"Yes, she is. I'm glad she's got two older brothers. They may come in handy in a few years." Denny grinned. "She's ready for a nap. I'll park in my chair in front of my room next door if you'd like to have a cold one with me."

"Great, I'll get the kids settled and be right out."

Twenty-five minutes later, while Raine and Thea played in the pool and Tyler made like a monkey on the climbing equipment in the play area, Jesse listened while Denny explained the ins and outs of the activities.

"Barnacle Bill's Minigolf is a big hit with the kids."

"I missed that last week, but I got to the dinner at the Captain's Table at The Sands. That was good."

"Yeah, I struck gold with a couple of the ladies," Denny responded with a smirk. "Farren and I were in high school together. I've been here all week, seeing my family." He made a face. Clearly, family time wasn't high on his agenda.

"You're a local then?"

"From across the bridge in Summerville, but close enough. The motel has the facilities for the kids and gives me an out when the family stuff gets a bit much. Everyone has an opinion, and they can be loud when they want to state it." He shook his head and Jesse wondered what drama had overtaken his neighbor and his family, but he didn't ask.

From Denny's attitude toward the "ladies," he'd bet his family had opinions on Denny's recent divorce. Jesse didn't want to get into the story, so he focused his attention on Tyler.

"Now, there's a piece I wouldn't mind getting with," the other man said quietly.

Jesse tracked Denny's gaze to Eva, who sat guard over the pool. Farren was still busy handing out information packets and another male staff member was putting hot dogs and burgers on the grill. The scent of grilling meat wafted by and reminded him how long it had been since he'd eaten a light lunch. "Do you mean Farren?" he asked because it was clear Denny wanted the question.

"No, I had that years ago. Check out the lifeguard. Sweet bod, right?"

He shouldn't be surprised that Eva's sleek good looks would interest a man like Denny, but still, his skin crawled. "She seems like a nice woman. Good with the kids." He bit the inside of his cheek to keep from telling the hound to back off.

Eva climbed down and knelt to talk with a child who looked about Tyler's age. She pointed to the pool and made swimming motions with her arms. The girl smiled and nodded and stuck her thumb in her mouth.

AS EVA'S GLANCE ROSE from the water, she caught sight of Jesse, sitting with Denny, a hound of the first order, who'd gone through several of last week's single moms. There was history between Farren and Denny, but her friend wouldn't elaborate beyond the fact they were once high school sweethearts.

She tried not to look their way again, but by the time she was on her chair, high over the pool, she couldn't focus on much of anything. Farren waved the last of the families toward their room and she approached Eva. "We have another request for swim lessons," she said. "He's four and his name is Tyler."

"Okay." Eva swept her gaze around the pool, proud that she'd ignored Jesse, who hadn't taken his eyes off her since she took to her chair. "I wish he'd quit doing that," she said.

"Who?" Farren scanned the pool to see the infraction. "No one's running or diving."

"Jesse's watching me."

Farren glanced his way, but Denny had taken his attention and her friend missed Jesse's heated glance. "You did spend *significant* time with him on the weekend," Farren said with a saucy grin.

When Eva grimaced at the comment, Farren cleared her expression. "It's natural that he wouldn't ignore you. I'm sure you'd hate that." She spoke gently as if to tread carefully around a touchy issue. "He booked last minute and when he got here, he said he'd enjoyed himself. He was sure his children would love it. You remember that last week he wanted to check out the activities before bringing them."

"I remember. And now he's here." *With his children.* She also remembered him chatting up the mom Cassie, then claiming they were in the friend zone.

"That's right. Will this be a problem for you? You said you didn't want to talk about your night with him, but if he's a problem, I can refund his money and ask him to leave." As the words tumbled out, Farren's voice grew fierce, as if she suspected something bad had happened during Eva's time with Jesse.

Eva patted her shoulder in reassurance. "He's fine. He doesn't make me uncomfortable. I'm the one who's made too much of this. Of course, he'd want his children to come along and have a wonderful weekend with new friends."

"Not to mention, he's an eligible single father and may want to find a permanent relationship. You've turned him down so he's back and keeping his options open. I hope he finds exactly what he's looking for." Farren eyed her a moment before checking with the teen in charge of the grill.

Of course Jesse was here to take part in all that Singles' Fest had to offer. He'd spend the days of the weekend with his children having fun and his evenings with a woman who didn't cut and run at the first sign of children. Jesse Carmichael was a perfect client for Farren. He and his children deserved every happiness and if Singles' Fest brought him that, then who was she to whine about it?

But she had her own children to consider. Her girls were missing her as much as she missed them and the worry gnawed at her every waking moment and most of her sleeping ones, too.

She had to focus on Sophie and Jilly and on her plan to try for regular video chats on Wednesday evenings. The scent of grilled hotdogs filled her nose, and she noticed a general exodus from the pool as parents called to their children to dry off for the picnic-like atmosphere.

The smiles and laughter made Eva sigh. Farren had done a good thing here.

Two of the moms walked by Denny who was seated alone now. He gave them a salute and a big smile. They stopped to talk. Soon, they smiled and laughed with him.

During her conversation with Farren, Jesse must've slipped away, leaving Denny on his own. Not that it mattered, Denny was on the hunt for women. Abandoning that view, she scanned the center court and found Jesse holding hands with his adorable, curly-haired boy.

He looked about four and his sisters ran to him and his father and called his name. Tyler. *Great. Just great.* She'd be teaching Jesse's son to swim. Her heart sank.

Chapter Seven

"Can we have hot dogs, Dad?" Thea, the younger of his girls, asked.

"*May* we have hot dogs, and yes, you may," Jesse corrected automatically, hearing Lynne's voice in his head as he reminded them of her one grammar peeve. "They have burgers on the grill, too."

"Let's put our towels on the grass and have a picnic," Raine suggested, and pointed to an empty spot on the lawn near the office. Several picnic benches dotted the grassy area.

A picnic would get him away from Denny and his deplorable commentary on the women who'd come to Singles' Fest for a good time. The guy was a jerk and Jesse was sorry they'd been put next door to each other, but his reservation had been last-minute. He was stuck.

"A picnic sounds like fun and that's what we're here for." The kids cheered at his announcement which made him feel like a hero for a brief shiny nanosecond.

The Landseer Motel was at full capacity. Good for Farren's business, but a shame for Jesse, stuck with Denny for a neighbor. With any luck the other man would be in hot pursuit of women most of the time and wouldn't bother with Jesse.

"Have you met the boys who are in the next room to ours? They're around your age." Maybe their children could make friends, though.

"No, we haven't met any of the kids." Thea was the quiet one and less likely to approach strangers, even children. He raised his eyebrow at Raine.

She shook her head. "We played with each other. It's been a long time since we were swimming."

He glanced at the lifeguard stand, but Eva was gone. Just as well, he didn't want his neighbor to figure out how interested he was in her. To Denny, Eva might be a prize in some twisted ego- boosting game. He'd met plenty of men like Denny. Men who kept invisible scorecards on the women they'd hooked up with.

Thea and Raine chatted happily a few feet ahead of him and he wished again for a woman in their lives who could help explain the male species someday.

EVA DRESSED QUICKLY in serviceable denim capri pants and a lightweight pullover hoodie. She gathered her belongings for her ride home. As she stepped outside, Farren and Grady called to her. She strolled to the grill where Farren held out a burger on a plate. "I got you one. The next batch won't be ready for a few minutes."

"I thought I'd pick up fish and chips at the J Roger on the way home."

"Why pay for dinner when we have this for you?" Grady asked. He indicated a small table and chair set waiting for them by the breezeway that separated his private home and the motel units. On the table sat a bowl of potato salad and a green salad topped by colorful heirloom tomatoes.

"Okay, thanks." Since they'd be sitting apart from the families, she could share a meal with her friends. They applied their favorite burger toppings and headed to the table to sit together. She sat with her back to the wall and her gaze fell on Jesse and his children. A pang hit her square in the chest at sight of his beautiful daughters.

Where were her girls right now? Preparing for another weekend visit with their nasty cousins? Her stomach rebelled at the idea. She set her burger down before her first bite.

"Are you all right? You look pale." Farren turned her head to look over the crowd. "Is it Jesse? Every time you look at him, you change. Earlier you looked strange, but now you look ill. If he did anything to hurt you—you don't have to tell me what—I'll ask him to leave and get him out of here."

Grady put his burger down, too. "Say the word and he'll be gone in fifteen minutes, and he'll know not to show his face here again." His voice had taken on a protective growling tone that warmed Eva's heart.

She shook her head. "I promise that my feeling off has nothing to do with Jesse Carmichael. Honest. To prove it I'll eat my burger, some of this wonderful salad, and then go join him on the grass. His children look delightful, and I suspect his boy is the Tyler who wants to learn to swim." She could talk to the child and make him feel comfortable before they got into the water together.

Easy. Any sane woman could do that.

Jesse and his children waited in line to get their hot dogs and burgers and then took their turns at the condiments table. The taller of the girls helped her brother with his mustard, which drowned all evidence of the hot dog in the bun.

Eva controlled a grin. Sophie loved mustard just as much as Jesse's son.

The other girl gathered their towels and took them to a patch of unoccupied grass. Most of the families had opted to use the available picnic tables. Farren had brought in extra-long tables so families could buddy up and share; anything to encourage new friendships. If her clients didn't find true love, they'd leave here with great memories and new friends.

Jesse balanced two plates while his daughter kept her hand on the boy's shoulder as they made their way to the circle of towels his other daughter had laid out. They settled with crossed legs and began to eat, laughing and smiling and...being the family she'd lost. She blinked to clear brimming tears and picked up her plate.

"I've changed my mind, I'll go join them now," she said and walked over to where they sat.

JESSE COULD HAVE FALLEN over when Eva approached with a full plate. "May I join you?" she asked, directing the question to his children.

"Yes," came the reply to her request in triplicate. Tyler bumped over closer to Jesse to give Eva room on their towel.

She'd changed into jeans that ended just below her knee and a long-sleeved pullover tee that sported the Singles' Fest logo over her heart. The color was a similar blue to the motel's roof. He wondered if the echo of color was deliberate.

"You're the lifeguard," Thea said, curiously.

"I'm also the swim teacher and I believe someone here asked for lessons. Could it be you young man?" She gave Tyler an exaggerated curious face.

Struck dumb by the attention, Tyler goggled at her.

Jesse took pity on his suddenly shy son. "This is Tyler and yes, I signed him up for a lesson. He'd like to learn to float so he can take more lessons when we go home." Then he introduced himself as if they'd never met. "I'm Jesse Carmichael and these are my daughters, Raine and Thea. Pleased to meet you."

She played along and did the same thing.

"I'm eight and Thea's seven," Raine offered with a happy nod.

"I saw that you both already swim really well."

Jesse caught her sympathetic glance but frowned it away. She turned back to the children. "Water baby classes," she continued. "That's a great way to learn. But Tyler will catch up quickly," she said with a grin at his son. "You look very strong and brave. I'll keep you safe and soon you'll be a very good swimmer too."

"Okay." But his thumb went into his mouth, like it often did in new situations.

"Thank you for reassuring him." He slipped his palm to Tyler's shoulder.

"That's why I came over to join you. I thought Tyler might like to meet me before the lesson." Her gaze skittered away from his as she focused on Tyler. He grinned around his thumb and then pulled it out of his mouth with a wet popping sound.

Jesse nodded. "You've already put him at ease."

Thea and Raine seemed to accept Eva at face value and while he felt a niggle of guilt for not saying he'd met Eva before; it was for the best. Since they were finished in the romance department, his daughters needn't worry about a relationship that was already history. Too bad he was the one having a hard time accepting it. But he'd admit defeat if he became absolutely certain it was over.

Raine spoke up. "This is called Singles' Fest, and there are lots of moms with kids and dads with kids. Is this a dating thing?" she asked Eva. "Like those swiping apps? Because my friend's mom goes on those. She says some of the men are real jerks."

Jesse's bite of burger turned to ash in his mouth. "Which friend?" He asked around the lump of food. He couldn't help it, the question popped out.

"Emily."

He swallowed hard and stared at Eva to see if she'd answer the big question while he fielded this bit of news about Emily's mother. "Her mom's a nice woman. I'm sure she'll find someone who isn't a jerk." Emily's mom had been one of the more desperate women to appear at his door after Lynne's passing.

Later, he'd ask if Emily had shown Raine pictures and profiles on the dating apps. His head spun with what she may have seen.

Eva cleared her throat and indeed, answered the bigger question. "Singles' Fest is designed to let parents with lots of things in common meet each other in a family setting." His chest warmed with her kind, easy reply.

Thea looked around at the happy children and the smiling adults who chatted enthusiastically or laughed together and nodded. "Like this?"

"Exactly." Eva went on, "If you find new friends here, you'll be happy you came. Your dad and all these other parents would feel the same way."

"I guess." But Thea narrowed her eyes at him, and he saw the exact moment that she understood what the weekend here meant. "You want to meet a lady, Dad?" Shock tinged each word. He should've discussed what the weekend meant before they came.

Tyler, oblivious to the undercurrents as both his sisters glared at Jesse, announced he wanted a bag of chips like the one he saw on a picnic table. He rose to his feet and wandered toward a snack table that sat in the middle of the picnic area. Jesse kept a close eye on him, but he did nothing more than touch a single serving bag and turn to look back for permission to take one. Jesse nodded and held up three fingers with one hand while he pointed at the girls with the other. Tyler grinned and picked up two more bags and returned. But when he sat down, he piled the bags in his lap rather than handing off the extras to his sisters.

Thea and Raine plucked their bootie right out from under his covering hands.

He scrunched his face but didn't complain.

Meanwhile, Eva watched the antics and gave Jesse an amused glance. Smoothly, she turned the conversation to the activities the children had to look forward to, forestalling more questions about the single moms Jesse might meet.

But he knew as sure as the sun shone every day, he was in for a grilling by his girls later.

Thea had asked if he wanted to meet a lady, and his heart answered that he already had. But things being as they were, he may have to suck up the disappointment and look elsewhere. He'd chatted briefly with a woman last week and it had been easy and uncomplicated because she was focused on her children while they swam and he'd still harbored hope that Eva might change her mind.

After the conversation with Cassie last week, he felt certain he'd find more women equally nice and interesting. He wanted someone genuine and when a woman chased after her kids there was nothing more honest. No one could be at their best under those circumstances. There'd be no fancy clothes or hair or make up. No false dating expectations that set everyone up for failure.

He warmed to the atmosphere and grinned to himself.

"That's a mischievous look," Eva said quietly.

"I was thinking how much fun we'll have this weekend. Every adult here will be both at their worst and their best. It's refreshing and way more interesting than swiping based on a few words and a picture."

Thea watched him closely. "Maybe Emily's mom should come here."

Eva responded. "Maybe she should. I'm sure when people get tired of those apps, tired of the phony people on there, they'll find Singles' Fest."

Thea nodded but still looked uncomfortable. "But my dad brought us here to have fun, not to find somebody to date. He wouldn't do that. He's happy just with us." The last was said firmly and Eva sighed under her breath.

This girl broke her heart. To Thea her dad belonged to her mom and that was that.

Chapter Eight

"Of course that's why dad brought us here, silly. Why else?" Raine lowered her voice, but Jesse found her tone harsh here in the dappled sunlight on the grass in the center court of The Landseer. "He wants to meet a single mom and make us like her kids."

Thea's face went ashen, and tears threatened. "He can't *make* us like them. Because we won't."

"That's enough," Jesse said firmly. "We'll discuss this later, I promise. For now, we'll finish our picnic and let Eva get on with her evening. I'm sure she has other children to talk to about swimming lessons." He tossed her a look that asked for support.

"That's right, I should move on," she said, and rose to her feet. "Tyler, it was lovely to meet you and I'll tell your dad when we can have time in the pool."

"Okay!" He exclaimed with breathless excitement around a mouthful of chips. Jesse didn't have the heart to warn him he'd spewed salty bits out of his mouth.

She looked at the girls. "Raine and Thea, thanks for letting me join you. I'll see you around the pool." She nodded to Jesse. "Nice to meet you. Tyler will be in good hands, don't you worry."

"It's me I'm worried about," he muttered with a glance at his daughters. "If I go missing look at family first," he quipped.

Eva included them all in a wave before she turned and walked away.

Time to face the music. The stone-cold expressions on his daughters' faces told him he was in for a hard time.

POOR JESSE. THAT CONVERSATION had gone sideways fast. Eva made her way to her scooter and stowed her backpack on the rack, stuck her helmet on, and climbed aboard. She felt for him, pinioned that way by two determined girls. Like a bug on a collection board he'd be stuck until they jointly decided to release him.

Raine seemed older than her eight years, but then, she'd been the woman of the house for some time. Eldest daughters felt the brunt of responsibility for younger siblings at the best of times. But having a widowed father brought an added burden. It was natural for her to think things through when events affected the family.

Her father bringing them to Singles' Fest counted as an event and affected them all. Big time. Clearly, he hadn't discussed the idea behind the weekend. The girls should have been told what to expect and that their dad might be making women friends. They were old enough to understand the concept of dating and remarriage. Thea already had a friend whose mother was using dating apps and spoke freely about her experience.

A pang settled in her belly at the idea of Jesse actively looking for a life partner.

Logic told her the idea for Singles' Fest was sound. She believed in its purpose. Emotionally, she wasn't sure she wanted to see Jesse enjoy success this weekend. Maybe if he'd waited a year since sleeping with her, she'd be better equipped to watch him chat up other women, but this seemed too soon.

Give your head a shake. She should dismiss all thought of the Carmichael family. It was Jesse's decision to explain to his children. Only he knew how to talk with his kids about his future.

With all she still had to do to launch *NanaBanana* and trying to stay in touch with her own daughters, she should put an end to her feelings around Jesse. It was over. Done.

Ending things had been her choice and he'd clearly decided to move ahead with his life. He'd been a distraction for her; nothing more. She should be pleased that he realized it and accepted her decision.

She skirted a pothole and focused her attention on steering as she put-putted her way home to Rook's Nest Cottage. She'd attempt a phone call with the girls before their bedtime. Maybe she'd get lucky, and Estelle would be out or ask Bernie to answer.

Half an hour later, her call was answered. "Hello?" It was Sophie! She was rarely allowed to pick up. Her grandmother must be unavailable.

"Sophie, it's Mom. How are you, sweetie?" Her heart clutched at the question.

"We're fine. How are you?" Her voice sounded stilted.

In the background, she heard Estelle's voice asking who called. "Sophia, answer me."

"It's my mom," she said, her voice distant as if she'd turned her head away from the receiver.

"You know that's not right. If your stepmother is calling, then it's unexpected. She knows not to call this close to bedtime."

"I want to talk to her," Sophie's voice went firm. Eva cringed inside because Estelle wasn't above grabbing the phone out of her hand. "And she wants to talk to me. To us." And then, "Jilly!" she called, "Mom's on the phone. Come say hi!"

The next glorious thing Eva heard was the sound of Jilly in the background. "Momma!"

From Estelle there was silence although she must be standing by listening. Amid a chorus of *I love yous* and *we miss yous,* the woman's heart might soften.

They managed a full five minutes of conversation during which Sophie and Jilly shared the receiver. Eva imagined them with their heads together as they talked over each other and then at last realized they needed to take turns to hear or have their say.

"Maybe we can have a video chat next Wednesday, like we did two days ago." Eva floated the idea in a soft tone, hoping Sophie would pick up on the need for quiet plans.

"We'd like that, Mom. We'll try," Sophie responded in the same tone. *Good girl.*

"Your grandpa will be in charge then," Eva hinted.

"That's right." Her daughter sighed, sounding relieved and Eva's heart soared. She'd made a tentative plan and Sophie was old enough to understand the significance.

"Good girl. I'll talk with you and see you both on screen then." She let her smile leak into her voice. "Good night, sweet dreams. I love you so much," she said.

"We do, too. Good night, Mom." Then she heard distantly, "No, she hung up already." And the line went dead.

Sophie had denied Estelle the chance to speak with her. Her daughter had protected her from Estelle's biting remarks. Sophie was growing up way too fast if she had to commandeer a phone and control an old lady.

Eva turned off her phone in case the woman called back.

JESSE SAW FARREN WAITING at the last hole at Barnacle Bill's Minigolf. He watched Tyler's efforts at rolling his golf ball by hand up to the whale's mouth. With a quick toss that no one was supposed to witness, his son got a hole in one.

"Yay! Tyler!" Thea and Raine cheered, completely going along with the illusion. They were good sisters to let him have his moment of triumph. It might not always be this way as he'd witnessed last night.

His daughters could be relentless interrogators when they were after information.

Farren waved him over as they cleared the way for the next golfers. As they approached her, she held out red tickets torn from a roll. "Who's ready for ice cream?"

"We are!"

"Who needs coffee?"

"I do," he said with a grin.

"Yuck," said Tyler.

"You can thank Farren and head over to the snack bar together."

"Thank you, Farren," they said and skipped toward the line for ice cream. Other children greeted them amid chatter about who won their games.

Jesse accepted the ticket for a coffee while Farren greeted the people behind him.

When the other family moved off, he spoke. "I commend you on the way things run so smoothly. We've had a blast. The girls made friends in the pool this morning and Tyler's having a swim lesson later today. Eva was good to squeeze in time for him."

"I'm glad. Eva will be sure to get him comfortable in the water before you go home."

He hesitated for a moment while Farren watched him expectantly. He ran his fingers through his hair. A nervous gesture that Lynne had recognized. Heat rose in his face, but Farren hadn't known him long enough to read him the way his wife had. He dropped his hand. "Speaking of Eva, has she mentioned anything about me? This weekend or maybe last weekend?"

"She did." Farren deadpanned.

"Care to elaborate?"

"Not my place, Jesse." Still expressionless.

He frowned. "Not gonna lie, I had hopes for something between us."

"I gathered," she responded softly, her gaze sympathetic. "She's a dear friend."

He nodded. Farren wasn't the kind of person to tell tales or swap gossip. Which meant she could be trusted. He took the leap. "I admire her, and I believe she likes me, but she's firm about not seeing me, about me not wanting what I want." And yet, she looked unhappy when she saw him talk to one of the moms in the group.

Farren furrowed her brows and gave him one brief nod. "It's generally a good idea to let smart people come to their own conclusions."

With that enigmatic statement, Farren moved on to the next group of golfers who clamored for tickets for the snack bar. When he turned to join his children, he saw them take a seat at a table with another family. He waved and the mom, a strawberry blonde, smiled in welcome.

She had one boy with her. He looked younger than Tyler by a few months or so.

He held up two fingers. "Coffee?"

"Thanks!" Her smiled widened. "Black, one sugar."

He nodded and placed his order. Two paper cups in hand, he joined the chattering children and set their coffees down. "As promised, but I can't speak to the taste. The pour looked weak to me. Coffee shouldn't look like tea."

She sipped, made a face, and said, "I'll just leave this here." She waved a hand to indicate he should sit across from her.

"I'm Kyley. This is Brent, who is three and a half."

"Nice to meet you, Kyley. Jesse Carmichael." He offered a hand, and she shook it, pleased. He named his children, who said hello to her.

They filled each other in on the basics. Fifteen minutes later, he knew Kyley was single, never married, and worked at a television station. She had a podcast on the side aimed at working single moms, and she had a good following. She was funny, sincere, and enjoying the Singles' Fest experience.

She put a finger to her lips after telling him about her time here so far. "I plan to invite Farren to join me on my podcast. My audience would love to know about Singles' Fest."

"I'm sure they would and Farren would be happy to talk to you."

"You know her?"

The question launched him into a description of how he and Archie had met Farren and Eva and how the men had offered their insight.

Her pretty green eyes widened as she listened. "You mean some of these ideas came from you?"

"Honestly? No, but I encouraged the ideas she had for making it easy for people like you and me to sit and talk and get over the awkward first date stuff."

Kyley rolled her eyes. "How easy was it to wave you over and have you join me?"

"How easy was it to offer coffee and sit down with you while our children are making nice with each other?" A glance down the table proved his point. Brent seemed taken with Tyler and listened with rapt attention to Tyler's explanation about tadpoles turning into frogs.

He and Kyley shared a happy gaze and then it hit him. He wanted this same easy-going connection with Eva. "I've already met someone I'd like to connect with. Have you?"

"Maybe." She smiled softly. "He has two boys. Seems nice. Doesn't live far from me, which is a bonus. He shares custody so he's not a full-time dad." She tilted her head, looking for more information from Jesse.

"I'm full time." Her honesty and directness were refreshing and prompted him to say more. "The woman I've met seems reluctant because I have the children all the time."

"Run."

The single word gave him pause. "But I saw how much she likes children." He blew out a breath. "It's weird."

"Then ask her. Is it the fact you have three? Or maybe it's something in her own life that makes her hesitate. I chat with lots of single moms and there are as many reasons to avoid dating as there are to try it."

"I'd love to have this conversation with her."

Kyley reached across the table and patted his hand. "Then do it. At least your mind will be at ease."

"Did you meet your guy here?"

She nodded. "On the viewing deck last night. One of his boys is in a wheelchair. They were watching the surf." She leaned in to speak without little ears perking up. "Brent had to inspect the chair and ask a bunch of questions."

Jesse could imagine. Tyler would have exploded with interest. He controlled a smile. "I'm sure the family's used to questions."

"It broke the ice, for sure. Mike's a nice man. He wasn't sure about bringing his boys here today, so we've got a date to come back tomorrow. It will be less crowded, and his son will be able to play without holding up too many other people."

"Sounds wonderful."

"I hope so. I see potential."

He wished he could be optimistic too. But Kyley was right, he and Eva had at least one more conversation to have.

Chapter Nine

E va watched as Farren packed her clothes to move them into Grady's house. "Jesse seems to make friends easily," Farren commented absently. She pulled a sundress out of the closet and laid it on the bed. "I saw him chatting with Kyley Mack at Barnacle Bill's earlier."

"Oh? That's nice. She's got that adorable boy, Brett." She gave her friend a smile that she hoped was breezy, but probably wasn't.

"Brent," Farren corrected her. "He's three and a half and every bit of it." She pouted then went on. "I believed Kyley had made a connection with Mike Smith, but maybe Jesse's more her type. He's certainly handsome and...interesting."

"He's also a good dad," Eva said quietly. One of his best attributes, next to his good looks and kind heart and intelligence. "Maybe he and Kyley will hit it off."

"I hope so, he deserves a good woman." Again, Farren kept her tone vague, but Eva caught a sly glance from her friend.

"Stop baiting me. It won't work. I *cannot* get involved with him."

"Not even for a good time? No strings? Just for fun?" Farren put her hands on her hips and offered a saucy grin and Eva wished for a nanosecond that she was free for a no-strings good time. "You did spend some quality time with him."

Her friend was fishing for more information on what happened between Eva and Jesse that night. But Eva didn't take the bait. "I'm not that person and neither is he. We both have children to consider. And that night was definitely a one-time thing."

Deep concern flashed across her friend's face. "The whole night?"

She caved. It might help to share the truth. "It was a mistake. Now he assumes we may have more between us than we do. But I can't go down that road."

"I'm sorry, I didn't mean..." Farren palmed Eva's shoulders and drew her into a hug and Eva allowed it. Needed it. When she backed away and looked into Farren's face she saw no judgment, just concern. "Have you made any headway with seeing the girls?"

"Some." Relieved to be on another, safer topic, she went on. "I believe I may have regular video chats on Wednesdays. For as long as we can manage it."

"Things will change for you; I'm sure of it." She tilted her head. "Meanwhile, I won't mention Jesse again, I promise."

With any luck, she'd be able to get Tyler to float and get comfortable in the water in one session and she'd never have to think about Jesse Carmichael again.

SHE COULDN'T QUIT WATCHING Jesse watch her. He sat on his chair in front of his unit after dinner and never took his eyes from her as her session with Tyler in the pool came to a close. He could float, hold his breath under water, and dog paddle a short distance. The boy had been more than ready to learn. She kept him in the shallow end, within view of Jesse and his daughters.

This lesson wasn't only the end of her teaching the boy, it also signified the end of any reason to speak with his father. She gave a silent thank you and focused again on Tyler.

Eva lowered her arms slowly and allowed Tyler to float on his back before he realized he'd been released. Around the pool a collective breath was held as the few people not at the beach playing volleyball and badminton, watched the boy's triumph. "Am I doin' it?"

Eva stepped back and raised her hands in the air so Tyler could see them. "You're a champ," she crooned for his ears only.

He flipped to his stomach in a commendable imitation of a seal. She readied her arms to grab the boy if he flailed, but instead of succumbing to fear, he rolled back up to face the sky. Then he stood and cleared the water from his face. His smile made the waning sun look dim.

A cheer went up from the witnesses that were now on their feet, Jesse included. She looked over at him and his pride made her smile back. She gave him a small wave, nothing noteworthy, but he deserved to see a response from her.

He picked up a towel and brought it to the pool. "I'm proud of you, Tyler." His gaze skimmed hers and then held as he silently thanked her. She smoothed her hands across her head and down her hair and squeezed water out of the strands as she went. "I'd like a word with you, Eva, if I may."

"Not a good—."

He cut her off. "Please. Just a few minutes."

"Okay," she walked toward the steps that lead out of the pool and rose from the water. He passed her towel to her, and she wrapped up. Cooler air blew in from the ocean as the sun continued its descent. "But don't you have to get Tyler to bed?"

"The girls can make sure he has a bath and gets into his pjs. We can sit in front of my room. I'll be right there." He pointed to the two empty plastic chairs that waited in front of the window.

"Fine," she muttered.

Other parents called to their children and soon, the center court would be quiet without the sounds of children at play.

"I'll go change and be right back. May I offer to bring you a soda? We don't keep beer in the break room. We have teenagers who use the room, too."

"Sure, I'd like a soda." His teeth flashed in a relieved smile that took her breath away and she turned on her heel and headed into the break room to dry off and change. She'd planned to shower at home, although Farren had told her to make herself comfortable and use the facilities.

Showering here would add time to her ongoing internal dialog where she had one conversation with Jesse that cleared up all the reasons she had for refusing to see him. And that would be the end of it. Under the hot water, she laid out her conversational approach.

JESSE'S HEART PICKED up its pace as he watched Eva walk toward him. Dressed in a soft-looking skirt that billowed around her calves, a loose pink cotton shirt with the tails tied at her waist, and a smile, she held a can of soda in each hand. One look at her and his goal switched from having an easy conversation about the children and tomorrow's activities, to getting her to agree to see him.

His focus sharpened as she stepped near, but she faltered as she looked into his face. He forced a benign smile. He was no longer Jesse Carmichael, easy-going widower willing to walk away from the best woman he'd met since Lynne.

He was a man in full pursuit of the woman he wanted more than his next breath. He almost told her to buckle up, but he didn't want her to raise her walls.

"Thanks for the soda. I checked on the kids and they're watching Tyler like hawks. They're also good big sisters who listen to his minute-by-minute account of how you taught him everything you know and that he's now an expert swimmer."

She laughed, as she was meant to and he watched her settle into the chair beside him, unaware of his new determination.

"He asked me more than once if he was the best student I've ever had." She crossed her legs and pumped her sandal-clad foot in an easy rhythm. "Of course I told him he was. He's four and they need to hear those things at his age."

"You're a natural with children," he said blithely.

"I like them," she admitted for the first time to him.

"Anyone can see that," he murmured before he took a sip of his cola. "That's why I don't understand how you can deny what we have might lead to something." He set his palm to her forearm where it rested on the arm of the chair. "Please explain your choice. I need to understand it better because, to be honest, I can't stop thinking about you."

"Jesse, I have good reasons. Two of them, actually." She opened her soda can and took a sip. "I've told myself that you don't need to know any more about me. But I see you look at me and I want to look back. I want to be with you, and I can't deny it." She shook her head and her gaze flitted across his features as if taking inventory. He hoped she was because that might mean she cared.

"Talk. I won't interrupt."

She looked at her lap, breathed deeply and sighed. "I'm a widow with two daughters. I married their father after his first wife died. I regret, with every breath, that I didn't insist on adopting Sophie and Jilly, but Rhys avoided the topic. Unbeknownst to me, he'd already given full custody of the girls to his in-laws in the unlikely event of his death."

Ice raced through his veins. "They have your children?"

She nodded but still looked at her lap. "I became their mommy when they were very young. Sophie barely remembers her mother, and Jilly was an infant. They're my babies, and they've been with people who hate me for six months." She fell silent and the only sound was his raspy breathing.

He let outrage grow until he wanted to stand up, run, kick something. Anything to expend this dark energy. "Do you see them?" His voice came out a growl of outrage.

"I'm not sure I can talk about this." The pain in her voice, the abject misery that seeped from her body into the gathering evening, made him reach for her hand. He stopped because he couldn't chance that his children would step outside and see.

"You don't have to say anything more. I can hear your heartache, feel it coming off you in waves."

She shook her head and then raised tear-filled eyes to meet his. "You gave me exactly what I needed last week when we were together." Her face reddened. "And it wasn't just the sex."

He nodded. "You needed to forget. To hide from this disaster." He stood up, turned around and faced the door stupidly because he had to move. Then he sat down again because, really, there was nowhere else to be. "How long has Rhys been gone?"

"It was a year on July Fourth."

"The night we...?"

She nodded. "He was driving to meet us at the fireworks. He was in a hurry. His last words to me were, 'come hell or high water, I'll be there.' Rhys loved fireworks, the bigger the better."

He swore softly and in deep sorrow. Sometimes life seemed impossibly cruel. "How long before they took your girls?"

"The Morgans told me in my kitchen, on the day of the funeral, that they had the agreement and the right to take them. She wanted them that day, but Bernie, Estelle's husband had more compassion." She tilted her head as if she still had trouble believing.

After a long moment, Eva continued. "I didn't believe it would actually happen, at first. I couldn't process what they said. The girls were upstairs, hiding from the sad faces in the house. They'd cried for most of the day. Clung to me through it all. Their grandmother's not a demonstrative woman and Rhys was only her son-in-law."

"Also, she was already plotting to take your children." Her girls were grieving hard but at least their grandfather showed them mercy at the time.

Eva pulled in a breath through her nose. She shook her head. "Estelle didn't need to plot at that point, she'd already done it when her daughter passed. Rhys agreed to the custody agreement while he was grief stricken. Of course, it made sense at the time. He was alone with an infant and toddler daughter to raise."

He wanted to ask why she hadn't adopted the girls, but her ragged pain stopped him. Still, a picture of her husband had formed. Rhys had signed off on his children in the midst of unimaginable pain with no hope of a happy future. "I understand your husband's mind at the time of his wife's death. I've been there myself."

He hoped he sounded understanding and calm and all the things she needed right now, while inside he raged.

"I can't blame him for agreeing at the time, but later? When I asked to adopt them, he put me off and I let him." She looked off into the middle distance, clearly reliving her saddest days. "Estelle and Bernie bided their time but when they reminded me a couple of weeks after the funeral, I found a lawyer. There was little we could do. Estelle and Bernie had used one of the best family lawyers in the city to draw up the custody agreement. There was even a clause in it about his remarriage. My husband signed it because he wanted to ease their grief by agreeing to never allow a new wife to adopt. He was a kind man with a big heart and when we married, he refused to discuss me adopting the girls because he claimed he couldn't hurt Estelle and Bernie that way. He said they'd already lost their daughter and the odds of him dying young were negligible. Maybe he'd forgotten about that remarriage clause or maybe he understood they'd fight him tooth and nail if he wanted to remove it." She turned haunted eyes to his.

"And now?"

"They've retired and moved to Summerville, presumably to get as far away from me and California as possible. Plus their son had moved to Summerville a couple of years before."

"But you weren't giving up." It was a statement; bald, powerful, and he applauded her determination.

"I sold the house, left my job, and moved to Last Chance Beach to be close to Sophie and Jilly. I'll open my daycare and try any means to get through to Estelle and Bernie that it's cruel to keep me from the girls." She chewed her lip and looked battle weary. "I just want regular visitation."

"You're their mom."

Her voice came out hollow. "I'm their mom. But I have no rights."

"They're terrible people," he muttered, more to himself than to Eva.

Her hand crept to sit on his knee. "No. I don't believe that. I can't allow for the idea that Sophie and Jilly are living with awful people." She choked back a quiet sob. "They're grieving their daughter and they want to hold onto her children. Rhys is gone and I was the interloper. As far as they're concerned, I have no connection to their grandchildren."

"Did you keep them away from Estelle and Bernie when Rhys was alive?" Maybe this was revenge.

"No. They lived two hours away and once a month, we'd drive them for an overnight. They called frequently and did video chats. They were well-connected and loved the girls and Jilly and Sophie loved—love—them. After they moved away, they didn't expect me to follow, and it threw them when I showed up here seven months ago."

"They assumed they'd won."

"I guess they did." She shrugged and looked inches smaller than she had when she'd sat in the Adirondack chair. She'd sagged into her frame, weary, frightened, but determined.

"I don't know what I can do to help you with this." But he'd find a way. "Tell me about them as people. What's Estelle like? Bernie?"

DID SHE WANT TO DO this? Talk about the people who took her kids? It would be easy to demonize Rhys's in-laws and make them sound horrible. Especially Estelle, who was the one she usually butted heads with over the girls. She shook her head and sighed. "They reacted to two terrible events by grabbing onto the girls. I get it. It's only human to want to hold on tight. I wanted to do that, too, but they were taken from me."

"Was the taking traumatic for them?"

It had been too sneaky to be immediately traumatic. Simple, really. "It wasn't a dramatic event. They weren't dragged away screaming." She closed her eyes to relive their last hugs. The last time she'd buried her nose in their hair. "I'd taken them to visit as usual and then, their grandparents kept them." Simplicity itself. "I showed up to get them and they weren't home. For days they ignored my calls."

"I'm sorry."

She nodded. "When Sophie and Jilly concluded they weren't coming home, they called in tears. It was horrible to hear them and be helpless. That's when their landline was cut off. Since then, I've only seen the girls a couple of times in person. And that was before they moved to Summerville." They'd only lived with Estelle and Bernie for a month before they left the state.

"So they got full custody and moved them across the country."

She nodded. "That's right. I assume they were stunned when I followed, but the only thing in California for me was memories. If I want to make more of those with the girls, I need to be here." Simple. And yet, nearly impossible. *Nearly.*

His hand crept to sit on her knee in silent support. She patted it twice, then settled her palm over his fingers. Comfort oozed over her, and they breathed in tandem.

"There's one bright spot," she said. "Bernie's softer than Estelle. On Wednesday evening, I'll try another video chat when Estelle's out. Bernie let us do that last week and I'll see if he'll make it a regular thing. If he'll allow regular chats, he may soften a bit more."

"Small steps," Jesses murmured. "I hope you get all you wish for. I'd do anything to help. Believe it."

She did. There was a set to his jaw, a gleam in his eyes, which spoke of deep emotion. Any parent would be touched by her story, but Jesse looked as if he'd taken it personally. But then, he had motherless children, too and had learned the hard way how precarious life could be.

Chapter Ten

W*ednesday – 7:30 p.m.*

Eva ended her video chat and sighed with contentment. The girls had been happy to see and chat with her. She hadn't truly lost them. They were just apart for now.

Bernie had come through and had allowed Sophie and Jilly to talk to her. She sagged against her headboard and let happy tears flow freely. Things weren't perfect, but this one small victory had them going in the right direction.

Sophie had confirmed that her cousins were still difficult, but she'd become tougher and had stood up for herself and Jilly. Her uncle had overheard a small bit of what his sons were saying. Then he stayed listening as Sophie spoke up. He let her say her piece, then stepped into the room and hauled the boys away for a stern lecture.

Jilly had giggled at the recounting. Of course, they'd followed their uncle and cousins and stood outside the den door to eavesdrop. He'd blasted them for a long time, went over what he'd heard and given them the definition of bullying. They'd sobbed when they realized what they'd been doing.

Sophie had sniffed in derision when Jilly said their cousins had learned a lesson. But she promised to keep on standing up to them. Beside her, Jilly had nodded solemnly.

Eva hated that her daughters had to deal with this alone. She called Bernie and when he answered right away, she collected her thoughts.

"I heard," he said before she could start the conversation. "I heard about my grandsons and how my son handled things. He called us when it happened. How long, Eva? How long have they been mistreated at their uncle's house?"

"I believe it started shortly after we married. Me being their stepmom seemed to be the trigger. Maybe they assume all stepmoms are bad. That's a common enough idea." Did the millions of loving stepmothers and stepfathers have this same battle?

A silence from Bernie, but he was a thoughtful man. He didn't speak without due consideration and when he spoke, he meant what he said, unlike his wife. Estelle reacted without thought and blurted her every emotion. After a moment, Eva heard a deep sigh.

"Estelle may have contributed to their ideas," he said. "Not that she'd condone bullying, but she has her opinions."

Estelle had made it plain how she felt about Eva every chance she got, and Bernie was well aware.

Eva waited a heartbeat. "It's okay that she didn't approve of me or of Rhys marrying again. I understand she was shocked and felt it was too soon. But I loved him, and the girls. They needed me, Bernie. I needed them, too." She drew in a breath and tried not to sob. "May I please be allowed to do this chat on a regular basis? I'll leave it to you to decide whether to tell Estelle about the weekly contact."

Another long, long, pause.

"Wednesdays she leaves the house at six forty-five for book club. She comes home at ten or so."

She blinked, hardly believing her request had been granted. "Thank you. This means so much."

"This is for my granddaughters." His voice was gruff with emotion and then he ended the call. That was no surprise because Bernie had a lot to consider. For the first time since Rhys's death, Eva felt a glimmer of hope.

She rolled off the bed and padded into her kitchen for a glass of water. Checking for messages, she saw that for once, no one was looking for her or asking questions about *NanaBanana*. Word was out about the daycare opening and slots were almost full. If this kept up, she'd have a waitlist before the weekend was over.

In the days since she'd had her heart-to-heart with Jesse and had given him the unvarnished truth of her situation, she hadn't heard from him. The rest of the weekend had flown by, and she'd seen him chat here and there with several of the single moms. But not the same woman more than once. Clearly, he wanted to keep his options open. *Good for him.*

She was glad. He deserved a chance at happiness, and he wouldn't find it with her. What were the chances of lightning striking twice with a single dad? Nil.

But then, that's what Rhys had believed about him dying young. No chance.

She hadn't eaten yet and she pulled out leftover chicken for a quick stir-fry. Chopping her vegetables, she saw her phone light up before she heard the chime that heralded a video chat. Thinking it could be Sophie, she tapped the screen to accept and was surprised to see Jesse's face.

"Hi!" She quit chopping and held the knife up so he could see it.

"Whoa! Did I catch you mid murder?"

She turned her head to look at her knife. "And if I say yes?"

"I'll be there in the morning to help clean up and hide the body."

Eva burst into laughter and the sudden release of tension helped. "Too late, I'll have eaten everything by then." She turned the phone so he could see her cutting board festooned with chopped carrot, broccoli, and onion.

"Nice to hear you laugh," he said as she propped him up against her water glass. She went back to slicing her carrots. "I wasn't sure if I should call. But it's Wednesday and I've been wondering how things went."

"Bernie allowed me to chat with the girls and has agreed to make it a regular thing."

His turn to laugh. "That's great! Is he breaking a rule?"

"He's doing what he believes is right for the girls. They had a situation on the weekend, and I think he feels guilty." She put oil in her wok and raised her brows. There was no way she could stir fry and talk at the same time. "Allowing the girls to talk to me will be good for them and he's accepted it."

"Will you tell me about it now or cook your dinner?"

"Cook. I'm hopeful, but if Estelle learns about his leniency, it could be over. I want to bask in the happy while I can."

"I called to say that I plan to be at The Sands with Archie this weekend. The kids will be with my in-laws." His face looked optimistic and inviting.

"I see." There it was: the unspoken invitation to lose herself in him again. Did she need to? Want to? Of course she did. But she shouldn't. Wouldn't. Would she? "Have a good time with your friend."

He blinked. "I want to be with you, Eva. And I believe you want to be with me."

"I'll be busy with Singles' Fest again."

"I'll fish and hang out with Archie in the daytime. But in the evening, Archie will find his own company. You and I will be free."

"I'm hanging up now." But she smiled as she said it and he smiled back.

FRIDAY EVENING JESSE unpacked his bag in his room and hung up his shirts. Archie had dumped his bag in his room and headed down to The Sandbar immediately. They were across the hall from each other, and Archie had hinted that the fishing this weekend was less about the fish in the ocean and more about the fish on land. Jesse considered his friend's comment and wondered if there was a woman he was particularly interested in or if he wanted any available female. Up to now, he'd steered clear of the Singles' Fest women. Archie wasn't a man who wanted a permanent relationship. Two weeks was long-term to Archie.

He called Eva when he was unpacked, and she answered on the third ring. A small, tight cog eased in his chest. He must've had some level of doubt that she'd take his call. "Hi," he said. "I'm here. Where are you?"

"At home. They're doing the dinner at The Captain's Table tonight. Tomorrow is dinner on the beach. Farren had people stay the whole week and enough couples requested the beach on their own that she moved the schedule to accommodate them."

The beach dinner was a romantic setting where the menu was limited and by request. Couples had a table for two, with linen and lantern light on the sand. Meals were catered and served by staff from The Captain's Table. The tables were spaced apart for privacy. At the end of their time with Singles' Fest, it was a wonderful setting for romance and memories to take home.

He wanted, badly, to make memories like that with Eva, but she wasn't ready. If she needed the quick oblivion she'd taken two weeks ago, then Jesse would provide. He'd hate to find out she'd gone somewhere else when he wanted her in every way possible.

"I'm kind of busy with *NanaBanana*, Jesse. I need to get some things done over there."

"I'll help. What are you doing?"

"Nothing interesting, believe me."

"Look, I understand totally why you're gun shy about my kids. I can't imagine what you're going through. All I want is to hang out with you. My kids won't know, won't get attached. Weekends when I'm here alone, we can be adult friends."

"You mean you want to hide me from your kids?"

"Not in the way you mean. They'll make friends, they'll see me chat with moms, get comfortable with the idea of me dating on weekends they're with me for Singles' Fest."

"And if you meet someone you like a lot?" she asked.

"Let's talk about this while I help you do boring things at your daycare. We're wasting time on the phone."

"Twenty minutes," she said, and gave him directions.

Gratitude rose and he wanted to thank her, but she was already gone. Nothing was far away in Last Chance Beach. He quickly changed out of the clothes he'd traveled in and headed out to do boring things with Eva.

And he couldn't help but look forward to being bored with Eva.

Chapter Eleven

As much as Eva was an independent woman who'd soon run her own business; a woman who wouldn't need a man's help with her decisions about staff, or expenses or customers or anything else, she was inordinately happy to not have to do this work alone.

Screwdrivers were not her friend, but this thing in her hand was not a screwdriver. It wasn't a wrench. Not even close. Maybe Jesse would recognize what it was and what it was called.

She knew, sort of, what it was for.

Two taps on the door alerted her to Jesse's arrival. She flung open the door with a flourish and waved him inside. He slipped in trailing the alluring, light cloud of scent his wife had had specially blended. Eva closed her eyes for a second, sniffed, and hoped he didn't notice.

His handsome face lit up when he saw the mess of different lengths and shapes of wood strewn across the floor. "This is the boring work?"

He smelled too good, looked too happy to be with her, smiled too wide. Her heart warmed of its own accord. Jesse Carmichael had too much appeal to resist. She should have known she'd be distracted by him. *But that wasn't his fault, was it?*

She waved a hand toward the pile of bits, parts, and planks of wood. "Don't laugh, but I oversold it. This is not boring, it's frustrating." She toed a plank. "This set has defeated me. I started it last night, but gave up, hoping I could make sense of the instructions after a good night's sleep."

He narrowed his gaze as his eyes tracked the various pieces.

She waved the strange tool in the air to get his attention. "Do you know what this is called? The instructions say it's a wrench, but it doesn't look like any wrench I've seen."

"It's an Allen key. Used to put together do-it-yourself furniture sets, or toys. Lots of things." He said it with a serious expression, but one side of his mouth quirked up.

"Oh, thanks." He hadn't mocked her or made her feel stupid. Half her frustration melted away. "I have more of them. They're different sizes."

"So, this is a kit for something for the kids."

"A kitchen set. Cupboards, countertop with a stove top with dials that turn. There's a microwave that hangs under a cupboard and a fridge with shelving. It should last for years."

"The girls had a plastic one. This look much sturdier." He stood with his hands on his hips as he surveyed the planks and squares of wood. There was a bag that contained knobs and another full of screws of various lengths and sizes. The instruction sheet was taped to a white board on the wall. "It'll take longer to put together, too."

"It will be sturdy when we assemble it. I've procrastinated and it's past time I got it done." She couldn't allow a child's kitchen set to get the better of her.

"We'll finish in no time." His focus stayed on the various pieces of wood. She loved the way he seamed his lips as he thought. Then he stepped to look more closely at the instructions she had on the wall. "Good. I see how this works."

She raised her eyes to the ceiling and mouthed a silent thank you. "I'm glad you do, because it's making me dizzy."

"How about you hand me the pieces I ask for and we get started. Don't worry, you'll do as much of this as me. And the Allen keys will be easy to use, I promise."

"Okay, I'm in." She believed he was a man of his word, another thing to find attractive. She wasn't sure she could take much more of Mr. Wonderful and still say no. Her traitorous heart laughed at her logical brain. He got down on his knees and reached for the longest plank, and then dragged it closer.

"Pass me the bag of screws." He held out his hand like a surgeon asking for a scalpel.

She set the bag in his palm and settled in beside him. She tried to ignore that every time he moved, she caught a whiff of his scent while he focused on the job at hand

He did not sniff her. She'd have noticed.

She learned to turn the keys in the right direction, held the cupboard doors when he set them in the hinges, and installed the knobs. The fridge looked great and opened easily. They worked quietly and efficiently until the tiny, perfect kitchen rose before her eyes.

When the set was built, she gave him an impulsive hug and he held her close, pleased to be her hero. "Thank you, thank you," she said next to his ear.

"Do I get a kiss to reward my hard work?"

Her answer was to turn his head and give what he asked for. Deeply, and with longing.

When she pulled back, he let her go, but his eyes were just this side of heated. His smile was way past smug. He understood his effect on her. So much for being careful.

He looked at the box that sat against the far wall. "Did we miss something important?"

"My supplies for the kitchen. I'll stock it tomorrow. I have wooden milk bottles, a pound of butter, a carton of eggs and a selection of fruits and vegetables in bright colors."

"Pots and pans and dishes, too?"

"Yes. Everything."

"Take my picture," she said and handed over her phone. She posed beside the kitchen, propped her elbow on top of the fridge and gave him a happy grin.

"Sure, you can print this one and install it by the front door, but we both worked on it." He stood beside her, set his head next to hers and took a selfie with the kitchen in the background. "This is the real picture."

Then he kissed her the way she'd kissed him. "I enjoyed being with you, Jesse. I can't thank you enough for your help."

"There's nothing I wouldn't do to help you out. But now, please join me for a stroll at the beach. The moon's full and we should see well enough to walk without tripping over rocks or driftwood."

As if she could refuse. "Sounds great. If we walk near the resorts, there are lights aimed at the sand."

"I walked over here," he said. "Can you give me a ride back? Or should we stroll over?"

"If you don't mind riding pillion, I have my scooter."

"I'll manage fine if I get to put my arms around you." He waggled his brows and made her grin.

"Charmer," she said through a chuckle. "If we get drinks, they're on me. I need to thank you for your work here."

"Time spent with you isn't work, Eva." He tilted his head and looked at her with a sweet light in his eyes. "But you already know that."

She did. When she got to her scooter, she lifted the seat and pulled her spare helmet out of the storage compartment. "This should do."

He climbed onto the seat first, bracing his feet on the ground, while she perched in front. His strong arms wrapped around her middle and he snugged up against her back. She patted his fingers, started up and drove off with a broad smile. The breeze, the scent of the man behind her, the feel of him at her back. She could think of nowhere she'd rather be.

NanaBanana had only a few touches left to complete, and she'd be open for business. Satisfaction filled her. No matter what happened with Sophie and Jilly, she planned to live near them. Owning the daycare cemented her place in Last Chance Beach while living near their son would keep Estelle and Bernie in Summerville.

With time, the Morgans would come around. She had to believe that.

Jesse's warmth caressed her back and she toyed with leaning backwards into him but refrained. He might take her actions the wrong way and look for a signal where there was none.

No signals? Hah! She'd let him work with her this evening, had kissed him, allowed a selfie and even more kisses, and now she was headed to the beach for a romantic stroll in the moonlight.

Eva didn't often lie to herself, but tonight had broken records.

She didn't usually carry passengers, but the zippy scooter responded well and ate up the distance to The Sands.

They'd have uninterrupted time when they hit the beach and she planned to put an end to this budding friendship as soon as she could. He'd made it plain he wanted to sneak around on his kids but that felt wrong to her. And what about the single moms he chatted with? What would they think if they discovered an employee was involved with a client?

Oh mama! His arms felt like a haven, and she gave herself permission, just for the moment, to enjoy the feel of him as they trundled along Main Street to The Sands. When they passed *The Rum Runner Bar & Grill,* she felt his lips next to her ear.

"We can stroll the beach and head to The Rum Runner for a beer." His voice, deep and velvet, tickled her ear and a thrill shot to her low belly.

Inside she shuddered at the image she'd conjured. The bar was a loud, raucous dance bar and he might find an excuse to hold her close standing up. They'd be belly to belly, thigh to thigh, with their arms around each other.

"Good idea," she said against her better judgment. Forcing her mind to clear, she told her body it had no input on what might happen tonight. None. He wouldn't want to go to the *Rum Runner* after she said what she had to say.

She turned into the circular drive at The Sands Resort and found a spot to park designated for motorcycles. They removed their helmets, and she stowed his in the compartment, but left hers on the seat. Her little Italian baby looked especially cute between two hogs. She doubted anyone would want hers with its bright daisy designs overlaying the soft pink base color.

JESSE FROWNED AS EVA put her helmet on the seat of her scooter. "You don't lock it?" She was too trusting and sweet. But look where trust had got her? She'd gone along with her husband's lack of foresight and poor planning and now her children were gone. He tamped back the bite of frustration.

"It'll be fine. It's too distinctive for a local to take and the people who ride larger motorcycles and hogs aren't likely to want something feminine." Her happy expression as she looked at the peppy machine was priceless.

"You're right, it's the most pink, fun ride I've been on," he said and nonchalantly reached for her hand.

Eva hesitated when she saw his gesture, but he kept his hand out. He wiggled his fingers, and she gave a slight shrug as if realizing refusal seemed petty. When she slipped her hand into his, she twined their fingers.

She was suddenly skittish. He thought better of pulling her closer, much as he wanted to. He hoped she'd feel comfortable with his plan to see her on the weekends when he left his kids at home. Singles' Fest weekends would be about Raine, Thea, and Tyler having fun and making friends. He'd have friendly conversations with other parents and some great activities to share.

But these weekends without the children could be solely about Jesse and Eva.

They walked into the expansive Sands Resort lobby and when they ambled past a gift shop, she noticed a bunch of colorful scarves draped over a rack. She drew to a halt. "Oh, I should get one of these for our stroll. The air will be cool by the ocean, and my arms are bare."

"Or I could hold you close." The words slipped out. Any excuse to hold her.

"We need to talk. Buying a wrap is the best idea." She glanced at the rack, gently lifted a multi-colored striped one off and took it to the cash desk. She had her credit card in the cashier's hand before he could get his out of his wallet.

Whatever she had to say couldn't be good. She had reservations about his idea to split his weekends between 'date' weekends with her and 'kid' weekends. But she was willing to talk and that encouraged him.

To cheer up he decided those kisses they'd shared meant something.

The cashier snipped off the tags and' Jesse held up the wrap to drape over her shoulders. He smoothed it into place but resisted the temptation to nuzzle her ear. She tossed him a smile in thanks, and they continued.

The pool was lit from below the water and several loungers held guests sipping drinks and enjoying quiet conversation. He'd like to be one of those couples, sharing a moment, talking about the day they'd had and the morning they planned for the next day.

"It's beautiful out here," he offered, but Eva's only response was to quicken her pace.

When they reached the sand, she removed her sandals. He left his shoes beside the stairs on a rack the hotel provided. She opted to carry her sandals and use her other arm to anchor her wrap at her waist.

So, no handholding.

"We do have some things to discuss," he began, as he slipped his hands into his pockets. "When I said I'd like to see you on the weekends when my kids are with their grandparents, I didn't mean it to sound like it was just for sex. That night we shared was a one off, and I don't see us that way. A no strings fling isn't—."

"Please stop." She held up her hand. "It isn't that I don't like you or want to see you as a date. I need to focus on getting my daughters back into my life. That needs to be my main goal. Especially now that *NanaBanana* is about to open. By Labor Day the daycare will be in full operation and between that and Singles' Fest, I won't have time for a relationship."

"You want to spare my feelings." But he didn't want to be spared. He wanted to be part of all that concerned her. Silently, he acknowledged it was fast for these feelings, but he'd been overtaken by a tidal wave name Eva. The funny thing was, he welcomed the wave without reservation.

"Yes, I want to spare you and myself." She stopped walking and gazed up at him. Her eyes were wide, suspiciously damp and held warmth that seared him.

"You don't want me to get my hopes up about us." He wouldn't, he vowed silently, but he wasn't ready to quit yet. Not... yet. Not when he wanted her like he needed his next breath.

"Right," she murmured.

"There's only one thing to do then."

"Right. We need to agree not to see each other alone. Please continue to come to Singles' Fest. Tyler, Raine, and Thea had fun and you could meet someone special."

"Yes and no."

She tilted her head and looked adorably confused.

"I'll continue with Singles' Fest for lots of reasons, but what I was about to say is, I may be able to help with your situation with your daughters. It's a long shot and I don't want to say anymore." He raised his hands and squared his shoulders to hers. "I'm not a lawyer or in any way able to approach this from a legal aspect, but that's not what will make them change their minds, anyway."

She frowned. "Then how will you help?"

"By coming at this in the best, most effective way possible. As a human being, a father, a widower. It'll take time, but it might work." All he needed was information. "I have a request. If you don't help with it, I'll have to find another way to meet Bernie in a public place."

Chapter Twelve

ednesday, 6:50 p.m. – Rook's Nest Cottage

W Jesse's ruse had no possibility of success, but Eva appreciated his desire to help. He'd convinced himself that if he met Bernie Morgan, he could make him see reason and defy Estelle. He wanted to appeal to Bernie's emotions.

She agreed with Jesse that all legal means had failed. It was a very long shot, but she despaired of finding a way through this quagmire.

Somehow, she had to figure out how to give Jesse the opportunity he needed. No way would his plan work, but since she didn't have another one, she needed to give this idea a shot.

What Jesse didn't understand was that Bernie's emotional responses were dictated by his wife. Eva had explained to Jesse that Bernie allowing her Wednesday video chats was a huge departure for him. The man had been married to Estelle for over thirty-five years and had put her first every day. She should be grateful for what he'd given her, not be greedy for more. But her heart wouldn't listen, and either would Jesse.

Bernie accepted his wife's lead; an impossible habit to break. Sure, he'd bent the rules when Estelle wasn't home, but the moment any of them slipped and the truth came out, the video chats would be over because Estelle would end them.

She'd spent days and lots of sleepless hours pondering Jesse and his plan. He wanted to plant a seed in Bernie's heart that might grow into compassion. That compassion was supposed to give the older man the strength to confront his wife.

Eva couldn't see Bernie making that leap, but Jesse seemed determined that it could work. Desperation plagued her every day.

Soon, there'd be a new school year and the chance of Jesse's plan working after September was slim. He needed time for Bernie's compassion to grow. The sooner the better.

Eva pulled her laptop off the coffee table and onto her lap. Estelle should be gone by now. She made the call and connected with the girls right away. Seeing them smile back at her onscreen made her heart thud.

Words tumbled out of them both, so many, so loudly she couldn't hear. "Girls, one at a time, remember?"

They both nodded at her and when they took turns, it became easier. Their cousins had been much kinder to them since their dad's lecture. It turned out that their mother had liked Eva and once she explained the truth to her sons, the boys had gained new perspective.

"I wasn't aware your aunt liked me. She was nice when I saw her, but I assumed she was being polite." She was a quiet woman and Eva had taken her demeanor to mean she followed along with Estelle.

Apparently, the Morgan family had opened up about Eva and how she'd been a good stepmother and loved Sophie and Jilly as her own. Eva's heart filled with appreciation. She'd had no idea that the parents supported her. She filed the information away to use later.

"I'm relieved I don't have that worry about you anymore. I'm proud that you spoke up, Sophie and I'm pleased that your aunt and uncle liked me." Everything had been filtered to Eva through Estelle's dislike. But now, their aunt and uncle had been open with their sons about Eva and what the Morgans had done by taking the girls.

She motioned for Sophie to move the camera to encompass the room behind her and saw Bernie in his easy chair reading on his e-book reader. Good, he was engrossed in his story. She held up a sign and Sophie nodded as she read it.

"We've been at the playpark near Summerville Creek and saw some boys catch frogs in a pond." Great! Sophie had understood the hastily written note and had given her the information Jesse needed.

"You did? Did they chase you with the frogs?"

Jilly spoke up. "No! They let us see them in their buckets. But don't worry 'cuz they didn't keep them. I got to release them back into the water."

"That sounds like fun. Will you go back there soon?" She nodded vigorously to show them the answer she wanted.

"Yes!" Jilly exclaimed. Bernie glanced at the girls, pulled away from his book by the small shout of enthusiasm.

"The best swings are there, and we can climb the bars really high." Sophie nodded happily.

Both girls had inherited co-ordination and balance from their mom. She'd been in ballet for years. Jilly's appreciation for the natural world had come from Rhys. "Grampa says we can go tomorrow. Right, Grampa?"

Bernie glanced up again. "Sure, we can go after school tomorrow." He frowned and Eva held her breath. "Where are you talking about?"

"The playground where the creek is. You remember the pond."

"The frogs," he said with an indulgent smile and a nod. "Sure, after school."

Eva blinked and covered her mouth, nodding like a bobble-head. Jesse would be pleased but she was still leery. She gave the girls a thumbs up and hastily scribbled another note. *You will make new friends there. Raine and Thea and Tyler.*

THURSDAY AFTERNOON - *Summerville Creek Park*

Jesse spotted a lone man on a bench beside the playpark. The setting was perfect. Summerville Creek meandered through a valley full of trails. The biking was great, and the valley was used by hikers and dogwalkers. The creek flowed under a short bridge and widened out into a shallow pond before it narrowed again to continue its journey to the ocean.

The playground sat above the creek on a grassy plain. The pond couldn't be seen from the playground because of a ring of trees around the water. A piece of natural beauty in the middle of town.

Perfect.

The girls and Tyler beelined for the play equipment while Jesse sauntered across the grass with a bug-catching net and a bucket. He sat on another bench next to the older man and set his bucket and net to rest against the side.

By the time he'd settled into his seat, Raine and Thea had already begun to chatter with the other two girls on the play equipment. One— he thought it could be Sophie— was hanging upside down from the parallel bars.

He suffered a pang when he realized Eva couldn't be here like this, watching her daughters having fun and making friends. He waved when Thea glanced his way and then ran to the swings with the younger girl. Jilly, most likely.

The older man's head moved to track the girls to the swings, but his attention soon turned again to the e-reader on his lap.

Bernie looked to be in his late sixties or so, balding but with a grey fringe around the back of his head. A straw fedora sat beside him on the seat. But the breeze explained why the hat wasn't on his head.

Which told Jesse that Bernie would suffer sunburn so his granddaughters could have playtime at the park. Without prompting from him, Thea and Raine had already started conversations with the only other girls that looked to be near their ages on the play equipment. He hadn't told them to seek out Sophie and Jilly, instead had chosen to depend on their natural friendliness.

After a few minutes of 'hey, dad, lookit me' from Tyler who swayed on a horse on a thick spring, Jesse held up the bucket and net and called to him. His son couldn't compete with the older girls, but that didn't stop him from wanting to climb onto the parallel bars. His older sisters shooed him away, which drove Tyler toward Jesse. His face filled with indignation at being told he was too little to climb that high.

Beside him on the other bench, Bernie stirred and glanced his way. "That your boy?"

"Tyler. He's four. He wants to see the pond and the frogs he's heard about in there. But first he'll complain about being bossed by his big sisters."

Bernie nodded and smiled. "Of course. I'd have done the same at that age."

Jesse chuckled in agreement.

"Mind if my Sophia and Jillian join you? They like the frogs, too."

"That'll solve my problem of what to do about having three kids who want to do different things. I suspect if your two want to go to the pond, then my Raine and Thea will follow, and I won't have any problem keeping my kids within sight."

Bernie stood as Tyler arrived to slam into Jesse's knees. "Let's go! You promised the frogs would jump into my net. And tell Raine and Thea they're not allowed."

Bernie laughed and Jesse stood. "Girls, we're heading to the pond," he said and waved the net in the air. "Tyler here just invited you." He made a face at his son and Tyler took off at a run for the steps down to the path that led to the water's edge.

All four girls jumped off the swings and came running. The short walk downhill to the bank of the stream was all it took to have Bernie introduce himself.

"I'm Jesse Carmichael," he replied. "Pleased to meet you."

They spent the better part of an hour watching the net be passed back and forth as the five children shared. He and Bernie filled time with small talk about books and movies.

Jesse snorted as he saw Tyler wait patiently for another turn with the net. "They're on their best behavior. Normally, Tyler would hog the net and bucket. Or he'd yell and bluster to get it back."

"They sure are having fun," Bernie observed. "If you plan to be here again sometime, I'll buy the girls their own gear and we'll join you." They sat together on boulders placed strategically for sitting or walking down to the water's edge. A crane had flown off when they'd arrived, his quiet fishing spot overtaken by laughing children.

"Sure, I'd like that. It gets lonely sometimes for a guy on his own at the park," Jesse commented.

Bernie snorted. "Sometimes the grandmothers want to strike up a conversation, but my wife's enough wife for anyone."

Jesse nodded and grinned. "That's nice. Mine's been gone for a couple of years now and I wish I'd had more years with her."

"You're not just alone at the park then?" Bernie gave him a sympathy-laden glance.

Jesse shook his head.

"Sorry to hear that, son. That's rough. I'm not just their grandfather." He tilted his head toward Sophie and Jilly. "We have them fulltime. Our daughter passed, then their father was killed in a car crash last year."

Jesse swore softly in honest sympathy, for Sophie and Jilly and for Bernie and his wife. "One family shouldn't have that much loss."

"Daddy, I'm hungry. Did you bring cheese and crackers?" Tyler called over from the other side of the pond.

"Sorry, Tyler. I didn't." He looked at Bernie. "Lynne would've brought snacks. She was always prepared. I doubt I'll ever get this stuff right."

Bernie patted his knee. "Bring some tomorrow. We'll be here again."

"Then we'll be here, too. Nice chatting with you, Bernie."

"It was good for me, too."

On the way home he listened to what a great time they had, and how much fun Sophie and Jilly were. He couldn't wait to call Eva and give her his report.

After the girls went to bed, he took his phone out to his veranda that stretched across the front of the house. From here, with their rooms at the back of the house, the girls couldn't hear him on his phone, and he wanted privacy.

Eva answered on the first ring, as if she waited for him.

Chapter Thirteen

E va snatched up her phone and answered immediately. She'd waited for what seemed like hours. Of course she'd waited. She was terrified that Jesse would be found out. Even if this idea was Jesse's from start to finish, she'd be blamed if the Morgans learned of his deception and connection to her.

"How did it go?" she demanded right away. No hello, no smile in her voice.

"Before we get to the pleasantries," Jesse said through a light laugh. "It went great. Bernie's a good guy."

"I always thought so; until he stood by and let my children be taken." Like that saying about evil winning when good men do nothing. A huge sigh escaped her, and the quickly indrawn breath that followed told its own story. She wondered if she should put her head between her knees to keep from fainting, but her next two breaths seemed normal. "How are you otherwise? See? I can deal with pleasantries now."

Jesse chuckled into her ear, and she felt the reverberation to her toes. She liked this man, who'd taken a chance for her that she would never ask of him.

"I'm fine. Thank you for asking. You didn't tell me what great girls you have. They're athletic, friendly, and full of confidence."

"Their mom was in ballet, but Sophie and Jilly love to play sports. Were they on the parallel bars? The climbing wall?" They'd soon outgrow the short wall, but last year, they'd loved it. She'd wanted to take them to a climbing and trampoline park, but they'd been taken away before she could.

"All of that and more. There's a creek beside the park that widens out to a shallow pool with bullrushes and small fish, and frogs to catch. At work tomorrow, I'll slip out to buy a couple of nets and buckets so the kids can each have their own."

"Amazing. Thea and Raine and Tyler made friends with Sophie and Jilly?" Was it possible? She closed her eyes and felt a sting behind her lids. She would *not* cry. "Wait, you said Bernie's a good guy? Have you connected with him?"

"We like the same author and I'm lending him a book I read years ago that he missed. It came out before he discovered the series."

"He's a book pal?"

"Sort of. I guess. We were the only two men in the park with kids. It was natural to gravitate."

She narrowed her gaze and wondered how he planned to progress with this budding bromance. "When do you plan to tell him that we're—that we're—." Oh, she couldn't say they were friends, or *more*.

"That we know each other through your work at Singles' Fest? Or that you're Tyler's first swim teacher?" Jesse, giving her an out. The man had a kind streak a mile wide.

"Yes, that. Either thing. They're both true."

"I'll play that hand when we need it. It'll take a while." *Slow and steady*. She nodded at the thought.

"Now, tell me about my girls. Did they look happy?"

His replies were all she needed them to be. Sophie and Jilly were engaged, happy, looked fit. Bernie kept a good eye on them, and they obviously loved him. Tomorrow, they planned to meet at the park again and it had been Bernie's suggestion. They'd take snacks to share.

Jesse's report was all she could ask for and more.

Then why did it feel like heartburn was eating her alive?

Because she should've been the one with them. She should be taking them to the park, watching them grow, helping with homework, talking about life, and sharing, and boys, and love.

It should've been her.

"I'm due to call the girls. I need to keep up my regular phone calls through Estelle, so she doesn't catch on that I talk with them when she's not around."

"Good. That's good. Will I see you this weekend? I'll be at Singles' Fest this time. The kids loved it."

They'd made it clear they wanted to come back again. "Yes, you'll see me in my official capacity as lifeguard and babysitter booker." She chewed her lip, concerned about something else. "Please don't let your kids in on what you're doing at Summerville Park."

"I won't. I couldn't trust them to keep a secret." He paused and let a couple of beats pass. "Will I see you alone? I could get a sitter for the kids, and we could have time by ourselves."

"Yes," she said simply. when what she should have said was the opposite. "As long as we're discreet. Your children can't know about us." Everything she'd decided about not seeing him and not *liking* him went out the window.

"That's for the best," he agreed. "The truth will come out at the right time. And it will work out. Trust me in this."

She had her doubts, but this was the best she'd felt in a year. Where there'd been grief and hopelessness, she now felt the power of a new attraction, and a glimmer of hope that she'd soon be with her daughters again.

SATURDAY NIGHT – THE J *Roger*

With the Singles' Fest parents at the speed date dinner at The Captain's Table at The Sands Resort, Jesse had suggested they meet at the beachfront seafood restaurant away from prying eyes. With its barrel-based, glass-topped tables and high stools, it was fun, rustic but not child-friendly. In short, it was perfect for two adults who didn't want to be noticed.

She'd resisted being alone with Jesse until now because he needed to be with his children, too and, hard as it was to accept, he also needed to hang out with some of the single mothers. Eva didn't want to stand in his way if he found someone else.

Farren had mentioned that Jesse booked a sitter despite not signing up for a seat at the speed dating dinner. The offhand remark had been cool, but her eyes had danced with curiosity. Eva had focused on changing from her tank suit into her sundress and sandals and ignored the broad hint for more information.

For added privacy, she chose to take a table inside the restaurant rather than on the expansive deck outside. Not that Eva was well-known yet, having only lived in Last Chance Beach for under a year. But still, she wanted to avoid people.

She told herself it was self-preservation and not a desire to have Jesse to herself.

She took a seat at a table away from the window and waited for all of thirty seconds before Jesse walked in, windblown from his walk along the beach from the Landseer Motel. His gaze locked onto hers as he approached. He stopped in front of her and as she looked up into his happy face, he brushed his lips across hers.

His kiss was light, comforting and made her want more. And more again. If she didn't know better, she'd say she felt her lips plump from the touch of his.

"Hi," he said simply, as if they hadn't seen each other all day every day since Friday evening when he and his family arrived. But they'd kept their distance and avoided being alone. The glances between them had been electric. Excitement had risen with each stolen glance and shy smile. The temptation to find a way to be alone for a moment had ratcheted her excitement.

"Hi, yourself." She watched as he pulled his stool out from under the round glass tabletop and settled close to her rather than across from her. This way, they could touch, brush fingers, caress a knee, or nuzzle an ear. But she'd do none of those things, she vowed in silence. Not a one.

What he chose to do was beyond her control. A thrill rolled up from her belly to her chest and she looked forward to seeing what he'd come up with for some inadvertent touches. Jesse was great at that particular flirtation.

"The kids are settled with the sitter, Casey Washington," he explained. "They had a great time together before."

"Casey's a great kid and needs the work."

"I allowed them thirty minutes in the pool and Farren said the ice cream truck is expected to show up around six-thirty. I gave Casey money for treats, and I bet they won't notice I'm gone."

They ordered the restaurant's most popular meal and chatted about nothing much until their small glasses of icy beer arrived. Once it was unlikely they'd be interrupted by the server again, Eva started.

"I understand you're making progress with Bernie, but I'm afraid that Estelle will come with him to the park."

He shook his head. "Bernie told me she's not into watching screeching children running loose. Her words, not his. Also, she doesn't like that there's a pond and is nervous about it. She's afraid of water."

"That's why Rhys and their mom got Sophie and Jilly swim lessons as babies." She nodded in sudden understanding. "It was to appease Estelle, to set her mind at ease. The boy cousins swim, too."

"Seems so."

A memory surfaced and she chuckled. "She liked that I'd lifeguarded as a teen. Not that she ever admitted approval, but she fussed about the girls swimming unless I went with them." She'd been entrusted with their lives but wasn't good enough to raise them.

"Look, Bernie and I see eye to eye on a lot of stuff. He's becoming a friend. Plus, he read the book I lent him and already returned it. That says something about him." Jesse bumped his shoulder into hers and let it rest there. "Not everyone returns borrowed books."

The heat of his shoulder against hers banished the chill around her heart. "You're the best kind of man, Jesse Carmichael." And it hurt that they'd never have more than stolen moments like this.

She clutched his hand and pulled it down to rest on her knee under the table. "I have something to say. You must understand, please, how much is at stake."

"This seems serious," he joked to lighten her mood and she appreciated it.

She lowered her brows and engaged his gaze. "If. We. Get. Involved." She had his full attention now. "And this plan of yours works, Estelle could react badly when she learns about you and me. She could flat out shut the door on me ever seeing the girls, being part of their lives." No more video chats or phone calls or contact. "They could move away again."

Her heart dangled over a precipice with strings as thin as spider webs holding everything in place. "One wrong word from the girls will alert her. Or Bernie could let something slip about—."

"About a widower he chats with in the park while our kids play together. Because that's all he knows." Jesse shook his head. "Don't worry about them moving because Bernie never will." He turned his hand palm up and entwined their fingers. "He's put his foot down. They live in a nice home near the girls' school, and not far from their son and his family."

She reared back. "You've come a long way in a short time with him."

"Men talk, Eva. Maybe not about feelings, but a lot of the stuff around feelings. Like decisions made because of grief, but not *the* grief. We talk about actions we take caused by emotions. Because men want to fix things and that means taking action." He brushed his lips over her ear, and she felt a rush to her belly. "Bernie lives with a strong-minded woman and loves her, but that doesn't mean that when he puts his foot down, she ignores him. Mostly because he doesn't put his foot down often."

She had no defense because no one knew what really went on in a long-term marriage. Bernie and Estelle had worked out their differences years ago and they each knew when to take the reins and when to hand them over. She and Rhys hadn't made it that far. She'd acquiesced to Rhys's handling of most things.

"Maybe you have a point. I've seen other times when Estelle deferred to Bernie. Not often, but it happened."

"I want to help you."

"But what if...." She trailed off, trying not to let her fear get the better of her.

"Let me help. When the time is right, I'll mention that I'm a client of Singles' Fest and that it's time for me to date again. A week or two after that, I'll say I've found someone nice. Someone I really like." He squeezed her hand again and she tilted her head for another of his fabulous ear nuzzles. "We'll talk about another woman raising my children. Me with a new partner, a wife. I'll give him some perspective on the dynamic that you faced with Rhys."

"As long as you're talking in the abstract and not proposing to me right now, I can accept your timing."

"This is not a proposal." He shook his head, his eyes serious. "My only goal with these Bernie conversations is to open his eyes to what you and Rhys faced. Once he sees that, he'll have a different view." He raised his hands palms up. "I hope."

She nodded, astonished by how much thought he'd put into his simple idea, which hadn't been simple at all. Eva arched an eyebrow at him. "Have you had your family tree done?"

He blinked at the change of topic. "No. Why?"

"You must be a descendent of the Machiavelli family. You're more devious than anyone I've ever known."

He put on an expression of pure innocence. "But I only use my powers for good."

"That's a relief," she said dryly as their platters of fish and chips arrived. "This dab of coleslaw is the best I've had," she said as she pointed at it with her knife.

He tried the slaw and grinned. "You're right."

"How do you think Bernie will feel—I guess the better word is react—when he finds out why you befriended him."

Jesse shrugged. "If my plan works out, he'll be relieved. He's concerned about parenting teen girls in a few years."

"Is that so?" She cut a piece of the perfectly battered cod and speared it with her fork. "They'll be in their seventies then. He has reason to be concerned." The fish was delicious as usual; fresh, light tasting and the batter crisp. "Time isn't on their side."

"We'll have a talk about social media next time I see him. Ask him when he plans to give them phones and how he'll handle online bullies."

"Okay, now you've frightened *me*."

"He's their grandfather but he's in the role of father, so these are fair questions. I'm asking him man-to-man. If I talk about the hard parts of parenting in this cellphone internet culture, he'll have no choice but to consider how he'll tackle it. I hope he's taking my comments home to his wife."

She blew out a big breath. "Thank you for everything you're doing."

They settled into their meals for a few moments while she considered where and how they'd spend the rest of their evening. She knew what she wanted, and she figured Jesse wanted the same thing, but when they walked out of the restaurant, he didn't reach for her hand.

So she reached for his. When they got to the sand he pulled her into the shade from The Rock, away from prying eyes and listening ears. He pulled her hand up to rest on his chest and squared his body to hers. "I've already said that I understand about our first night together. But I repeat, that's not why I'm here with you. I want us to get better acquainted. To explore where this is headed. I want more than what you gave me that first night."

The man was stubborn. Devious, even. He made her want him even while refusing to accept what she offered. "There's too much at stake for me to offer you more."

"Then, we wait until the stakes are lower. We wait until we're free to be together openly. We wait until all our children know about us, until Estelle and Bernie and Sal and Tina know about us."

They could try, she supposed. "That's a long list of people you want approval from."

"That's not what I said. I'll take acceptance if we can't get approval."

"Acceptance has a nice ring to it." Life would've been better for everyone if Estelle had simply accepted her.

Chapter Fourteen

The Landseer Motel – Grady's kitchen

"Jesse's frustrating me." Eva said to Farren at seven thirty the next morning. For fifteen minutes she'd been attempting to write an email detailing what she wanted on her website. Instead of writing simple instructions to the designer, her mind wandered back over the night before.

"Men have frustrated us since time began. What's he done? Be specific." Farren's tone was amused as she poured Eva a mug of coffee from Grady's machine. She claimed he had the best beans and Farren had taken to grinding them fresh for each pot. Heaven in a mug.

"The coffee in the break room isn't half this good."

"Too many people make it so it's inconsistent." The rule in the break room was the person who took the last cup had to make the next pot. It was rare that anyone bothered to take the last cup. Often, the coffee was sludge at the bottom of the carafe. "So...what's up with Jesse?" Farren prodded. "You can't mention frustration and then not fill in the details."

Eva propped her chin in her hand. "There are no details. After that first night together, he's become adamant that we don't repeat it and I agreed because I thought, I *believed* that I'm not a no-strings woman. He wanted us to be friends and now things have changed."

She was botching this and felt so uncomfortable, she shifted in her seat. "I've tried to make him understand why I can't risk involvement with a man with children. Not again. It would kill me if we broke up. Especially if the children are as sweet and fun as Raine, Thea, and Tyler."

Farren nodded, looking facetious. "I can see why a really great guy who's a loving father with wonderful children could be a disaster. What sane woman would hitch herself to that train wreck?"

"That's not fair." Farren had crossed a line with her sarcasm and Eva closed her laptop. "You're negated what I've already gone through."

Farren's face fell. When her hand stretched across the table to cover Eva's, she looked contrite. "I'm sorry, I didn't mean to sound flip. Getting back into Sophie's and Jilly's lives are your priority. But is it wrong to be with someone new? Someone who obviously cares for you, and by extension, the girls you love?"

Her heart squeezed and Eva had a sudden, blinding revelation. "Jesse knows about my children; he knows the whole sorry mess that my life has become." *He was trying to help her.* She glared at Farren. "He's not the train wreck in this relationship. I am." She patted her chest for emphasis.

"And he still wants to be with you, to be your support, your friend, and to help you get what you most desire."

Confusion reigned while Eva covered her face with her hands and sobbed. "Oh, Farren, what will I do about Jesse?" What if everything he did for her failed? The what ifs rolled through her mind like thunder.

"Hang in there. See him when you can. Let him know if you feel like moving ahead with him. But if you definitely feel like you can't move ahead, then be firm and let him go." She snorted. "Sorry, that wasn't much help, was it?"

She felt silent as she thought. Her coffee had grown cool by the time she spoke again. "You're wrong. You were a lot of help. Perspective is everything. Thanks to Jesse, my daughters know his children. They're friends, even." She had a lot to consider, not least of which was Jesse's determined plan to get Bernie on their side. Because as much as she saw herself alone, Jesse was right there with her.

Farren smiled. "I'm glad. I want whatever is best for you. Now, how can I help with your website?"

Her mind clear, she smiled. "I can do it now." She opened her laptop again and the words flowed. She made a bullet list of requests, each point essential to have on the site. Her mind cleared and her confusion drifted away.

Jesse wanted more than a no-strings relationship and she was suddenly hopeful that she could give him what he wanted because she wanted the same.

The question was how to get it. She felt a lightness in her soul she hadn't felt since Rhys had proposed.

"Once these tweaks are added to the website, I'll be satisfied with it."

"Good. Then you can decide what you want with Jesse."

"Already done," she admitted with a cheeky grin.

SUNDAY MORNING AND Jesse planned on a stroll to The Sands for breakfast with the kids. He ushered them outside and turned to lock the motel room door.

"Eva!" called Tyler from behind him.

Jesse swiveled his head to see her step out into the sunshine from the breezeway that led to the motel owner's private home. He offered Eva a tentative wave. She was leaving Grady's place at this time of the morning?

Her smile as she strode around the pool to approach them broadened as she included Tyler, Raine and Thea. The girls said enthusiastic hellos.

Eva kept her gaze locked on his and a curious warmth spread through his chest. *What was she up to now?*

"Good morning, where are you off to at this early hour?" She made a show of checking her watch. "It's only seven forty-five. I thought Farren was an early riser, but you're just as early."

"Daddy's takin' us for breakfast," Tyler piped up. "Wanna come?"

She tousled his hair and smiled at Jesse, stunning him to silence. "I'd love to come along." She looked at the girls. "If it's okay with Thea and Raine?"

Jesse cleared his throat. "Works for me," he said, with a glance at his daughters.

"Sure!" Thea replied.

"Okay," Raine said with a shrug. As one, the girls turned to lead the way to the beach. "We're walking there, though," she tossed back over her shoulder.

"Great! I love to walk the beach. But this early, we have to watch out for land sharks." She fell into step beside Jesse.

Tyler stopped dead. "Whaaatttt?"

"Sharks that like to roll around on the sand before the tourists arrive." Eva said it blandly as if everyone had heard about mythical land sharks. "They're shy, though, so we may not see any."

Tyler frowned. "I don't believe in land sharks. Do you, Daddy?"

"Not at all, Tyler. But we'll look them up when we get back." He cocked an eyebrow at Eva, who kept a straight face.

"Okay, you can search the internet, but like I said, they're shy."

"Right."

By tacit agreement, Jesse and Eva lagged behind the children as they scampered toward the playground where they used the slide and climbed the bars while waiting for the adults to catch up. "You met with Farren already?"

She nodded. "We went over final details for my website. She's just been through all that with hers, and I needed advice. This was the only free time she had for me today." Eva smirked at him. "You noticed I came out of Grady's house? They may be getting more involved, but that's a story for another day."

"I noticed," he admitted. "But you forget I saw Grady lay a claim on her when we first met. He left no doubt where his interest lay."

"Aw, shucks," she teased. "Here I thought you might be jealous."

"Not of Grady." But he wasn't the only man at Singles' Fest who'd given Eva more than a second or third glance. Denny was the top of that list, but he quickly dismissed the man. Most of the women Jesse had chatted with had seen Denny for the hound he was.

His hand wanted to reach out for hers, but he controlled the impulse. "I'm more confused about what's happening here and now." He motioned between them. "You joining us for breakfast is the opposite of what you said you wanted last night." Maybe she'd had a change of heart since she'd pointed out the reasons they shouldn't see each other, not even in secret. That conversation had given him the worst night sleep he'd had in months.

"I got some perspective, thanks to Farren," she confessed. "Jesse, I appreciate all you're doing for me. I can't imagine another living soul wanting to help me the way you do." She pulled a corner of her lower lip between her teeth, in a gesture that made him want to kiss her.

His restless night had given him some answers too. "I relate to Rhys, wanting a happy home again. I relate to Bernie, being concerned about raising children years after he's done it once. I feel sorrow that you're missing your children. You may not have birthed them, but they're yours just the same. If I'm lucky enough to find a woman to take me and my kids, then I want her to be just like you."

Eva stopped in her tracks until he turned to face her. "Oh, Jesse, that's the sweetest thing you could've said."

"I want to kiss you, right now, right here." He hooked a thumb over his shoulder to indicate the climbing, laughing children. "But it's too soon for them."

"Way too soon. We'll take this slowly for their sakes." She gave him a mischievous smile. "But on the weekends when they're not here?"

"We won't go slow with anything." He thought about how that sounded. "Except when going slow works better than fast." He gave her what he hoped was a salacious look and then ruined it by waggling his eyebrows.

EVA GIGGLED AT JESSE'S attempt at seducing her with humor. *Giggled.* "I haven't laughed like this in far too long. I like it. And I like that you're the one that can make me let go this way."

"I am, too." He made to reach for her hand but pulled it back when Tyler shouted at them to hurry up.

Keeping a sharp eye out for land sharks, Tyler held her hand as they made their way toward the resort. It had been a long time since she'd held a small hand in hers and she cherished every moment.

The first time she'd held Jilly as an infant flashed through her mind. She and Rhys were planning a walk along the oceanside in Mission Beach near San Diego, and he'd passed the baby to her while he got the stroller out of the hatch of his SUV. Sophie was still in her car seat patiently waiting for someone to free her from her straps. Eva hadn't yet learned how to work the closures and snaps, so Sophie had to wait for her father while Eva held Jilly.

But the sweet-smelling roly-poly infant in her arms enchanted Eva and she'd fallen in love in that moment with Rhys, a loving daddy, and his children. In a matter of weeks he'd proposed, and their lives were never the same.

She became an expert in car seat duty, in hugging, loving, caring and in daycare drop off and pick up. She'd once been the queen of wiping noses, cleaning bottoms, bathing babies.

All because of the feeling she'd felt holding that tiny girl.

The very same feeling she had now as Tyler chattered about sea animals, both mythical and real, and held her hand with his sand-coated, warm, little fingers.

She was in love. Jesse and the girls were a bit ahead of them as Raine did cartwheels along the water's edge. Water flicked with every athletic move and Thea danced out of the way of the droplets. Jesse cheered them both as the small group made their way south to the restaurant.

She had a lot of relationships to sort out. But at least this one was clear. She and Jesse would give this a good shot, and she hoped his children eventually approved.

She needed to continue her efforts to stay connected with Sophie and Jilly and work on Estelle to accept her.

Maybe Jesse talking regularly with Bernie would help, too. Men sharing their life trials was a different kind of sharing than women did. She had to trust that in this, Jesse knew best.

Chapter Fifteen

Going out for breakfast reminded Jesse of taking Raine and Thea for pancakes with Lynne. They used to love whipped cream with a cherry on top and all the syrup they could get. Lynne had always asked for a bowl of strawberries for the table.

"Pancakes, girls?" He asked as they strolled into the restaurant and looked for a table near the glass wall. The view was spectacular and today the giant sliders were open to allow the salt air to freshen the wide expanse.

Raine shook her head. "I want fluffy eggs and two sausages."

Thea nodded. "Me, too."

They took their seats and Tyler sat next to Eva. "I want pancakes," he announced and glared at his sisters.

"No, you don't," Raine said with a stubborn set to her jaw. "You want eggs or cereal."

"Raine, your brother's chosen. Tyler, if you want pancakes, I'll order you some. With whipped cream."

"And strawberries," he said.

Eva patted his hand. "They're my favorite. I'll have the same." She smiled up at the server as the young woman approached. "But first, I'll order coffee."

"Two?" The server raised an eyebrow at Jesse. When he nodded she looked at each child in turn. "We have orange, apple, and mango juice. Or milk."

The children ordered and Jesse hoped that was the end of any disagreements. Tyler could react strongly when his sisters intervened. He had a strong sense of injustice when they denied him anything. But this time, the crisis had been averted.

"But Mom ordered pancakes and strawberries," Thea whined at Jesse. "She loved them."

Jesse leaned down to her ear. "And she'd be super happy to know Tyler loves them as much as she did."

Thunder crossed her features, but in the end, Thea nodded. "Okay."

Eva looked stricken as red infused her cheeks. Jesse gave her a quick shake of his head. They needed to move onto another topic. Eva nodded just as quickly back at him.

"Tyler," she said. "I'm going to wash my hands after being on the beach picking up shells. Would you like to wash up with me? There's a lot of sand on your hands."

Tyler shook his head. "I go to the men's room with Daddy." He held up his hands to inspect them and looked at his father.

Raine rolled her eyes. "He'd rather stay dirty than go with *me* now." She elbowed her brother and threw Jesse an expectant look.

Thea nodded in agreement. "Raine and I can stay here and take our turn when you come back."

Jesse shared a look with Eva. Raine was nine going on thirty and she was responsible and dependable. "They'll be okay as long as they stay in their seats." He firmed his tone and added, "And the server will be back any minute with the drinks."

"We won't move. We promise," Thea insisted.

As soon as they moved out of earshot, Eva spoke. "They seem okay that I'm here."

"They've hardly spoken to you."

"That's because Tyler was with me. They wanted you to themselves for a change."

"Sorry about the pancakes. That came out of the blue." He was sure things could've been worse, but Thea had controlled her tongue because Eva was with them. "Raine likes to be in charge, and expects Tyler to take orders, but Thea surprised me. I never imagined that she'd complain about strawberries."

"It's natural that Raine would feel responsible. It's also natural for Thea to want to preserve her memories of her mom."

"You're right. Thanks for understanding." He held the men's room door open for his boy. "Here we are, Tyler. Let's try to do more than just wash your hands okay?"

"I don't hafta pee."

"Try. I don't want to bring you back—."

THE DOOR CLOSED, CUTTING off the conversation between Jesse and Tyler. Eva made a quick turn to glance back to their table. The girls sat as if they were enjoying a formal tea service, stiff and proper. The server approached the table with the drinks.

Five minutes later, she took her seat and gave the girls a broad smile. "Mm," she said. "The coffee smells good." She poured a dab of cream into the dark brew. "How have you been? It's been a while since we shared that picnic by the pool. I see you around the motel, but we haven't had time to talk."

"We like The Landseer. But some of the ladies Daddy talks to aren't as nice as he thinks," Thea said.

At that bombshell, Eva found herself leaning closer. "Really?"

Raine took over the explanation. "Some of them yell at their kids."

"I see. Are their kids behaving at the time?" She hadn't seen anything that looked like more than general calling and correcting some rough behavior.

"No. Some of the kids are *really* bad. Like running beside the pool and stuff and hogging the swings and not letting other kids have a turn."

Eva pinched her lips together to keep from smiling. "This sounds pretty typical, though. Any time there's a lot of children playing, you'll see some kids be greedy, or bossy." Most children ran near the pool; it was hard not to. But a whistle blown dissuaded the running for a few minutes and the parents also kept a sharp eye.

Raine listened intently to Eva's opinion, then her gaze hit the floor. "That's true. It's like at school sometimes."

"Exactly." She looked from one sister to the other. "But you two have each other at school, which is good. You're lucky."

"Yes." Thea agreed and looked at Raine.

"Yeah."

"And Tyler has you to watch out for him, too. Even if he doesn't like it sometimes."

"Sometimes he's the one who won't get off the swing," Raine confessed.

Thea eyed Eva critically. "We know why daddy comes here. It's to find a lady to marry."

Jesse's younger girl appeared to be the deep thinker, and unafraid to voice her opinion. Eva nodded and considered the change of topic. "Maybe he wants to find a friend for himself and new friends for you."

Thea's expression brightened. "That would be okay."

At that moment, Tyler zoomed up to the table and jumped into his seat beside Eva, saving her from responding. He grabbed his plastic cup and gulped down a big drink of milk.

His father followed at a more sedate pace and took his seat across from Eva. His gaze met hers and a silent joy passed between them. He kept his eyes on her as he sipped his coffee, the mug covering the lower half of his face.

Jesse Carmichael had slipped in under her defenses. Heck, she hadn't known she needed defenses, because until him, she'd been numb to everything but the pain of her losses. Rhys's death and the loss of her children had dulled her, made her bereft.

Her only reason to get up in the morning was to find a way to have her daughters back in her life. Somehow, some way, Jesse had widened her scope. Being around him had opened her up to new purpose.

Maybe, from here, this place where she was able to share a joyful glance, a warm look, she could rebuild some of what she'd lost.

Maybe life was calling to her.

Maybe.

THURSDAY, SUMMERVILLE Creek Park

Now that Eva had finally agreed to see him and hangout with his children, Jesse was more determined than before to get Bernie's support. He climbed out of his vehicle while his kids followed. He walked to the open hatch and pulled out a bucket and several nets. They had a routine now; twenty minutes on the play equipment followed by a quick snack and then they hit the pond. Today was Bernie's turn to provide the snacks.

He pulled out his travel checkers board and headed across the park to where Bernie sat. Today was the day Jesse planned to open Bernie's mind.

After they'd played checkers for a bit, Jesse cleared his throat and looked off into the middle distance.

"Spit it out. You've got something on your mind," Bernie said as he studied the board.

"I told you I've been involved with a dating app."

"You meet someone? That's great." The older man looked up and smiled widely.

"It's an app that caters to single parents," he said and launched into an explanation of Singles' Fest. By the time he'd finished explaining the concept, Bernie had focused his attention on Jesse. The board sat between them on the bench, the game only half played.

"Your kids like this woman you've met?"

"Seems so. But I can't help feeling...disloyal."

Bernie moved a checker. "After our daughter passed, our son-in-law moved very quickly to replace her. He was lonely and Sophia was only a toddler. Jillian was still in diapers."

Jesse nodded. This dovetailed with what Eva had said. "He needed help. I get it. Tyler was born only months before Lynne was diagnosed. He missed out on a lot of time with her because of her treatments." All the tears, the disappointments, the battles she fought. Jesse blinked a couple of times.

Bernie nodded. "I'm sorry for what you went through, son." He cleared his throat and looked at his knees. "My wife never got over how fast it things happened with Rhys. Rhys was my son-in-law's name," he explained. "Estelle considered the new wife a leech. She never did reconcile herself to our granddaughters being raised by another woman. Called the whole affair indecent. I couldn't change her mind or get her to see things from Rhys's side."

"Are you saying I should go for it or wait until the girls are older? Because I've been alone for two years."

Bernie gave him a nod. "If you find someone who makes you and your kids happy lightning's struck twice. You need to grab on. How many people get a second chance at a happy home?"

Bernie said the same things he'd told himself five minutes after setting eyes on Eva. He hadn't been ready until he'd seen her. "She's a good woman," he told Bernie. "She loves kids, and she's happy to hang out with a guy with three children."

"This is a single parents' group? Does she have children, too?"

Jesse hesitated. It was too soon to tell Bernie all of it. "Two girls," he said. "They're close in age with your two." The truth, but not all of it. Not yet. He sure hoped he could hang onto this friendship when the whole of it came out. He enjoyed Bernie's company.

"If they get along the way these five are, I'd say you've hit the jackpot, son." Bernie's gaze swung to the play equipment. "Snack time," he called, and Jesse smiled in relief.

Chapter Sixteen

Friday evening – Landseer Motel

Eva and Jesse sat outside Jesse's motel room. The air was lightly scented by the ocean and the breeze was perfect. Other couples sat in much the same way as Jesse and Eva. Through the open door, the sound of a children's movie played while Jesse's children watched and giggled. Tyler made a running commentary as he explained the plot. His sisters never complained, used as they were to his need to sort out the story.

All around them, people chatted about their day, had a drink, and got acquainted. Some fast friendships had formed among the parents and since the first weekend a few relationships had begun. Those people had stopped coming to Singles' Fest events, leaving room for new families. Eva was sure Singles' Fest was a smash hit and she hoped she'd had a small hand in its success.

"I've told Lynne's parents that I've met you." Eva startled at Jesse's comment. She hadn't expected him to tell his in-laws about her yet.

"You have?" This news pulled her out of her relaxed reverie about Farren's success. Of course, Jesse would warn them that he'd met someone. Eva nodded and crossed her legs at the knee. They'd had another picnic on the lawn in the center court. This time, they'd picked up two pizzas, because Tyler didn't like spicy pepperoni. He'd had a four-cheese pizza and promised to have the leftover for breakfast. She let the thoughts distract her from Jesse's announcement.

But he wouldn't let it rest.

"No comment?" He asked as he held a bottle of water in his lap and gave her a sidelong glance.

"Your in-laws were okay with the news?" She kept her voice soft, as he had.

"Tina asked more questions about you than Sal did. She also agreed to say nothing to the kids. I'd like Raine and Thea to come to terms with it in their own time. Telling them I like you seems like I expect them to be happy about it. I don't want them to feel forced."

"You're a good man, Jesse. I fully agree. Sophie and Jilly were young when I came into their lives. Your children should approve of me before we reveal our relationship."

"They like you already. I'm sure of it. But they watch me closely when I talk with the single moms."

She knew that to be true, considering they'd complained about some moms yelling at their children. A quiet pair of thuds on the floor interrupted them. "Probably Tyler jumping down from the bed. He was keyed up and he doesn't like when movies end. He may need to sit with me for a bit."

"Maybe I should leave," she offered.

"Absolutely not. He'd see you leave anyway. Might as well be here with both of us."

Tyler stepped outside, his soft curls tousled and eyes wide with excitement. It seemed to Eva that he loved these extra moments with his father. "Tyler, the movie's over?"

He shook his head. "No. I want it again."

"Where are your sisters?"

"Sleeping." He peered around his father and saw Eva in her chair in front of the window. "Eva!"

His father lifted him up in his arms and then closed the door gently. The click sounded loud in the quiet of darkness, broken only by murmured voices and the faint lap of water in the pool.

The moment Jesse sat with him on his lap, Tyler squirmed to stand. His father released him and then he climbed on Eva's knee and rested his head on her shoulder. She wrapped her arms about him and sighed with the joy of the moment.

"One down, two to go," Jesse said with a grin. He smoothed his boy's unruly mop of curls and then took a sip from his water bottle. "Life is good."

"It can be very, very good," Eva agreed softly as she enjoyed the scent of baby shampoo and sturdy boy.

THE NEXT MORNING JESSE gathered his children for what was quickly becoming a tradition. They were dressed and ready for the day. "Do you know what you want for breakfast?"

"Tyler has leftover pizza," Thea pointed out.

Tyler scrunched his face into a mask of disgust. "I want pancakes with whipped cream and sprinkles." Apparently, the strawberries had been forgotten. Either that or Thea had pressured her brother.

He eyed his younger girl, but she looked unconcerned.

"You read my mind, Tyler," he said. "Let's walk down the beach and go to the resort for breakfast. Your uncle Archie will be there."

"Cool!"

As much as Archie denied liking children, he had a soft spot for Jesse's three. Always had. He had the honorary title of uncle and deserved it. He'd been there for every birthday, and every time Jesse had had to leave them to be with Lynne. Archie had held Jesse upright when he'd stumbled out of her hospital room after saying his final goodbye. Sometimes, Jesse wondered if Archie hadn't been halfway in love with Lynne himself.

Strolling around the pool at the resort, he spied Archie and Eva together at a table large enough for the whole group.

Raine stopped in her tracks. "What's Eva doing here with Uncle Archie?"

"She must be his girlfriend," Thea said thoughtfully.

Tyler didn't care about the why of seeing Eva, he just ran full tilt toward her. "Eva!"

As Jesse drew closer, Archie rose and offered a handshake. "Hey, having a good time?" his friend asked.

"We were until now," Raine said abruptly.

Archie frowned and Eva and Jesse shared a stunned look. "Raine, what's the problem?" Jesse demanded.

"Yeah, what gives?" Archie wanted to know.

"Are you trying to ruin everything?" Thea asked of Eva.

"What? Of course not. I don't understand," Eva responded as she settled Tyler between her and Archie.

Raine shot Jesse a glare.

Jesse shrugged at the two other confused adults. "Everything was fine, I swear. We walked over, enjoyed the surf and now this." He pulled out a chair across from Eva and sat. "Girls, we need some clarification."

"I'm sorry for what Thea said," Raine declared as she sat next to Jesse and looked across the table at Archie. Her eyes narrowed into what Jesse was coming to understand was his daughter's death stare.

"I'm not sorry." Thea announced and flounced into her seat with another glare at Eva.

The server walked toward them, and Jesse held up his hand. "Bring orange juice for the children and a round of coffees for us." The server nodded and turned on his heel, clearly used to family *discussions* at breakfast.

"Explain yourselves right now," Jesse said to the girls on either side of him.

"It's not fair," Thea began. "We want Eva to be dad's girlfriend, but she's here with Uncle Archie."

Raine leaned forward and reached across Jesse's chest to try to grab Thea's arm. "Shut up." Her face bloomed red.

Eva slapped a hand over her mouth as her eyes darted from one girl to the other, while Archie's mouth hung open in shock.

Shocked, Jesse shook his head. "I invited Eva here," he blurted into the sudden silence. His daughters blinked while his son shrugged and turned to look around at the other tables. He'd clearly already lost interest.

"Are you sure?" Thea asked suspiciously. She crossed her arms over her chest and looked like a trial lawyer. Chilling.

He kept his tone serious. "I distinctly remember calling her an hour ago. I think that means, I'm sure."

"Honest?" Thea relaxed her shoulders and her arms slid open. Poor kid had way too much going on inside her head. His Thea, forever overthinking. He gave her a fond smile.

Archie lowered his head to be at eye level with the girls. "Look, I like Eva. But not the way you think. I was walking through the lobby and saw her arrive. We came to the restaurant at the same time. We sat down together to wait for you. That's all." He nodded his head in solemn affirmation. "I promise." He ran his hand over his mouth to keep from laughing.

Jesse couldn't let the girlfriend comment go. "How do you mean my girlfriend? Explain what you think a girlfriend for me might mean to us as a family."

Tyler, silent until now, piped up. "Smooches and stuff. Don't you know that stuff Daddy?" His son gave him a look that emphasized his dimples and questioned his father's good sense. "And you can hold hands, too. And look goofy when you see her."

Jesse sank back against the chair. "Smooches," he said through a soft huff of air. "Are you girls okay with that, too?"

Thea nodded and Raine bussed his cheek. "We like her better than the other moms at the motel. They have kids, and we don't want other kids. Just us."

"We just want *her*," Thea confirmed. "No other kids."

EVA FROZE AT THEA'S adamant words. "No other kids," she repeated under her breath. *No. No. NO!* She tore her gaze away from the children and looked at Jesse. He paled while Archie sank into his chair, silent but for his labored breath.

Still, Archie was the first to rally. "Thea, Raine. You can't dictate who your father will like or want to spend time with."

"Uncle Archie," Raine said with a glare at him. "We like Eva the best out of all the ladies our dad has talked to."

"My friend has a stepbrother and he's a jerk," Thea said. "We don't want a jerk in our family."

Eva covered her mouth, refusing to cry out. She had to hold herself together. *Get a grip.*

Jesse drew in a deep breath. "This discussion is not appropriate here. I invited Eva to share a lovely breakfast with us and she obliged. We're friends," he said. "But we are a long, long way from talking about marriage."

"But we like her!" Thea insisted.

"Yeah," Tyler added.

Raine was silent and looked guardedly at Eva.

"Excuse me, please," Eva said quietly. "I have a headache. I need to go home and rest." She grabbed her handbag and rose. "I'll leave you to talk through whatever you need to say."

Jesse looked ready to spit nails and she barely controlled her quivering chin before she turned tail and speed walked out of the hotel. She didn't look back.

And she certainly couldn't look forward to a future.

Dear Lord, when would she learn to stay away from men with children?

HOURS LATER EVA WAS still stunned by the announcement from Jesse's daughters. They'd accepted her as a possible partner for their dad, but they were adamant that they couldn't accept other children into the family.

She wanted to tear out her hair. Why hadn't she and Jesse seen this giant pitfall? Of course, Raine and Thea had no idea that Eva was a package deal. Sharing their dad with a new wife was one thing but sharing him with other children was another. Of course it was.

Eva and Jesse had thought they were clever letting his kids choose Eva without being coaxed. But her supposedly child-free status was a huge part of why they liked her for their dad.

It was over. Whatever she and Jesse might have had was dead before it had breathed. She could not give up her children for someone else's.

Jesse had texted and called her, but she couldn't face him. Couldn't bear to discuss this new loss.

She'd come home, crawled into bed, and pulled the covers over her head. First, Rhys had died, then Sophie and Jilly and were taken and now her future had been yanked away from her again.

Children.

They could break your heart without on a moment's notice.

The doorbell rang. This was unusual in Last Chance Beach because most of the time it was a friend or neighbor, and they were more likely to knock or peer into front windows or walk around the back of your house to find you. Using the doorbell was formal and meant the person was on a serious errand.

She couldn't handle serious. Covering her head with her pillow, she blocked the buzz of the second ring.

Five minutes later, she heard a sharp rap on her bedroom window. She raised the pillow and peered over her shoulder to see Farren with her face against the glass, hands cupped over the top half of her face to block out the sun. "I see you, Eva. Open up."

"Fine," she grumbled under her breath. "But I don't want to talk," she called through the house as she made her way to the kitchen door. She turned the lock to the open position. "There, it's open," she said through the door. "Come in if you want."

She turned toward the coffee pot. This would be a long conversation. Dregs of yesterday's last pot looked like tar on the bottom. She didn't care.

Farren stepped inside.

"If you want coffee, you'll have to make it yourself." She crossed her arms over her stomach and wanted to sink to the floor, but her legs held her upright. She backed up to plant her shoulders on the wall and slid down, propping her head on her upright knees. With luck, the floor would give way and swallow her. That dreamed died as she sniffed and waited for a lecture on not quitting. To heck with that. She was so ready to give up, she tasted ash.

"I talked to Jesse," her friend began. "He told me what happened. He's worried about you, and I am, too."

Eva muttered about nosy friends who should mind their own business, but when she got no response, she decided her knees had blocked her muttering. She spoke louder but kept her head down. "Don't worry. I'm fine." She sniffed and looked up, no longer hiding her bloodshot, red-rimmed eyes. She must look like a zombie.

That would explain the half-dead part of her heart.

Farren picked up the glass coffee carafe and looked at the sludge at the bottom. She set it down again. "This isn't like you, Eva. You usually find a way around obstacles."

She nodded. "I know. But I've lost so much and now I've lost Jesse, too. And his children." She blamed herself. "I'll be fine. I just lost sight of my goal, got ahead of myself, wanted too much, reached for the stars. Take your pick."

Whatever, it was over.

"I don't agree. The things you want enrich our lives. You want a loving partner. Doesn't everyone? You want the children you were given to raise. Naturally, you do. I believe you can have it all. Look at everything you've done, what you've gone through, to have what you want."

Eva sank into herself, denying what Farren said. "No." She smoothed the wet from her cheeks. "In one breath, the girls gave their approval for Jesse and me to explore our friendship. Tyler said we could"—she hiccupped— "smooch and stuff. And then, in the *very next breath*, they took it away by announcing the only reason they'd allow it is because *I have no children*." She hiccupped again. "It's true, I don't have my children, and I may never get them back in my life."

Farren's stricken silence weighed down the very air in the room.

"It's time I accepted I'll never regain what I lost." Eva hung her head. With a deep sigh, she continued. "Sophie and Jilly will never come home to me. Jesse can't make his children want more sisters. And I was a fool to believe this might work." She'd been in a lovely pink balloon of denial, floating above her pain. Too bad it hadn't lasted longer.

Farren eased up beside her. "With time, Sophie and Jilly will be old enough to decide for themselves where they want to be. Stay in touch. Force it if you have to. Keep knocking on that door, and never give up."

Her only answer was a low moan of grief. But moaning wouldn't make Jesse's daughters accept stepsisters. His family life would go from functional and happy to constant discord because the adults were selfish. She refused to bring dysfunction to the man she loved, to the three new children that had stolen her heart.

"I'm sorry this worked out so wrong. But his daughters will come around. He told me they're already friendly with yours."

"I'm not sure why I went along with *that* idea. Bonkers, is what it was. When Bernie and Estelle find out about Jesse manipulating that coincidental meeting in the park, they'll probably accuse us of stalking.

They could get a restraining order or sic a lawyer on me. They use the legal system like a weapon." Especially against her. She couldn't fight them. "They'll see a terrible conspiracy where there wasn't one." She rung her hands, agitated. "This is bad, Farren."

"You told me Bernie has the softer heart and that he allowed your video chats. That counts for something."

"Wednesday evenings." She shuddered. "I hope he doesn't take them away." It was something. One small joy in this ocean of disaster.

"He may never find out there's a connection between you and Jesse."

"He won't if I stay away from Jesse. I need to break whatever connection Jesse thinks we have." She'd be brutal if she had to be. A clean break, sudden and absolute, was her only option.

Chapter Seventeen

Three days later – Summerville Park

Jesse waved and started across the park toward Bernie, relieved that the other man had Bernie hadn't come to the park for two days and Jesse had become concerned. They hadn't exchanged contact information yet and Jesse had worried that Bernie or the girls had decided not to come to the park anymore. "Hi there," he said with a broad smile. "I was starting to worry."

Bernie stood and offered his hand to shake. "No need. The girls and I wouldn't miss our time at the park unless forced to. I was needed at home." He took his seat again. "Estelle took a spill down the stairs and is laid up with a badly twisted ankle," he explained with a shrug. "I was chief cook and bottle washer for a few days. I'm only here now because she's getting better on her crutches and insisted she needed quiet time without the girls underfoot."

He wondered if that meant she'd stay home from book club on Wednesday. If so, he'd warn Eva as soon as he could. *If she ever answered his calls.* It had been three long days of silence.

"I hope Estelle's okay now," he said. An older woman falling downstairs was serious. "She didn't bump her head, did she? I'm picturing her black and blue." He shuddered to think of it.

"No," Bernie assured him. "She was carrying a basket of laundry, turned her ankle on the bottom step and she landed on her rear. Still it was a fright and a trip to the hospital to have it seen to. From now on, I'll be on laundry duty." He made a wry face. "I've been told not to mix colors with whites a thousand times already."

Jesse nodded. "When Lynne got sick, I learned that the hard way." He chuckled. "Then there's the heat setting on the dryer. That's a whole

143

other lesson with synthetic fibers." Behind him, the children chattered loudly, obviously delighted to see each other. He took his seat on the far end of the bench and cocked his head. "They're relieved to be here with their friends." He smiled, genuinely pleased to see the older man. Aside from his goal to eventually solicit Bernie's help, he'd come to like the man.

For want of a better term, they were buddies and shared things in common, like favorite authors, books, and movies. Bernie was full of good advice. Reasoned advice. He spoke from a life's worth of experience.

Bernie closed his book; a political thriller Jesse wasn't familiar with. "I can tell you it was a shock to see Estelle at the bottom of the basement stairs. I had a few bad moments going over the *what ifs*." He pinched his lips together and shook his head.

"I understand. Especially since you have Sophia and Jillian to consider."

"I honestly don't know what I'd do if I was alone in this." He waved a hand to indicate the giggling, cheerful children. "I'm not a young man like you." Bernie sounded emotional and a little frightened.

"Have you and Estelle talked about what will happen if either of you is left alone?" He needed to ask the question because he wanted to share the answer with Eva.

"Not yet, but we will." Bernie cleared his throat. "I've talked to my son, though. He and his wife say they'd take the girls if it gets too much, or we have health issues. But they made it clear they'd include the girls' stepmom in their lives." He frowned and shook his head. "I don't think we've done right by Eva. She loved—loves—the girls like her own. But Estelle was grief stricken about our daughter and I let this terrible rift happen."

Jesse had been careful, had never used Eva's name. This was the perfect opportunity to come clean. And he would, but first he wanted to understand exactly where Bernie stood.

"Rift?" he asked to encourage his friend to talk.

"When the girls' father was killed, we pulled out our custody agreement and enforced it. We took them from the only mother they remember." Bernie looked off into the middle distance. "I'm ashamed to say I let it happen and when Estelle wanted to move across the country to Summerville to be near our son, I hoped we were—I don't know what I hoped. Maybe I just wanted to keep peace with Estelle. She was broken about our daughter, our little girl."

"Bernie." Jesse reached to set his palm on the man's shoulder. "We've become buddies, here at the park." Bernie turned to him and nodded.

"I need to share some news."

"You can. Anything. It seems a day for confession."

Jesse smiled gently. "Good. You're right." He cleared his throat to give him time to come up with the right words. "I'm in a real jam and if I don't get this right, I could mess up a lot of lives. Including yours."

Bernie's brows beetled and he tilted his head. "As you've just heard, doing nothing, or going along with whatever doesn't sit right, can mess people up. Spit it out." His gaze searched Jesse's and he straightened his spine.

"If you could fix your mistake with Eva now, would you?"

He nodded. "Yes, I would. No, scratch that. I will fix things between us." A small lift of his lips said a lot. "I have no idea what you're about to say or how it could affect my life, but I hope you learn from my mistake. Deal with whatever jam you're in *now* before it gets worse. Your turn."

Jesse nodded and drew in a deep breath. "I told you I'm seeing someone I met through Singles' Fest."

"Right. You like her a lot. And if I'm any judge, you're hooked." He raised his hand. "Don't let this slip away. Grab on."

He wanted to do just that. "The thing is my kids like her a lot. Gave us their permission, in fact." He chuckled. "Tyler said it was okay if we smooched."

Bernie chuckled, too. "What more could a father want to hear?"

"The problem is that my kids have never met hers in the normal way. I did meet her through Singles' Fest, but she's not one of their clients."

"No?" Suspicion dawned in the older man's eyes.

"She lifeguards, gets babysitters for clients, and is a big help to the owner. They've been friends since she moved to Last Chance Beach about eight months ago." Jesse took a breath, wondering if his friend had worked out the information about Eva or connected on the timing. "She's opening a daycare center in a couple of weeks." He saw the exact moment the truth bomb went off behind Bernie's eyes.

"Eva." Bernie said, clearly shaken. "It's Eva. I've heard her talk about the daycare to the girls."

Jesse nodded. "I wanted to meet her daughters, to meet you, since you've been such a big help. Letting Eva video chat with Sophie and Jilly has meant the world to her."

Bernie blinked. "And to them. They look forward to Wednesday evenings all week. They save their news for their mother and nearly burst to tell her everything. I wish Estelle could see it, but I doubt she's ready." He squared his shoulders. "You engineered our meeting here. To what end?"

"I hoped you'd see the situation from Eva's perspective, but I believe now that you already do."

Bernie nodded. "I'm not an ogre and no matter what you may think of Estelle, she's not either. She's a woman who's locked in the anger stage of grief and she can't seem to move on. Eva has suffered the brunt of that misplaced anger." He sighed. "Where do we go from here?"

His using the plural "we" encouraged Jesse.

"Since she's not a client of Singles' Fest, Raine, Thea and Tyler have no idea Eva has children. One of the reasons they gave their approval of us, is because they don't want to add children to our family. They like Eva a lot, but part of that is because they assume she's not a single mom."

The other man's expression changed, his eyes widened and understanding dawned. "And Eva?"

"Hasn't taken a call or text from me in days. This is killing her. We thought we had something special. When my children liked her and approved, I felt I had my second chance." The words spilled out as he confessed. "And in the next breath they said they never wanted step-siblings."

Bernie nodded and looked like he'd aged ten years as he saw the mess Jesse was in.

"You've got a chance here to fix this, Bernie. Even if Eva and I are over, I want her to have her daughters in her life. Can you help me?" He stared into Bernie's shocked eyes. "Will you help me?"

Bernie stood and paced back and forth a few feet, clearly thinking deeply. "How? Estelle doesn't know you, hasn't met your family."

Relieved he hadn't been punched in the face, Jesse stood, too. "I don't know where this should go from here. But I love Eva and my kids do, too. She loves Sophie and Jilly, and they love her."

"I've never doubted Eva's devotion. When she quit her job and followed us here, I admired her for it."

"What did Estelle think?"

Bernie snorted. "She didn't talk to me for a week when I told her we'd made a mistake to assume Eva would give up. That the girls deserved to have her in their lives." He shook his head. "I'm afraid my wife is blind where Eva is concerned."

"You said your son and his wife sympathize with Eva."

"They do."

The children waved from the play equipment. "Did you bring snacks?" Raine called.

Bernie called back. "It was my turn this time."

"Yay!" Tyler yelled. "You bring good ones."

Bernie grinned and said, "Estelle bakes the brownies and when I told her Tyler doesn't like nuts in them, she started making two different types." He held out his phone. "Take my contact info and give me yours. Call me and we'll talk this out."

"Thanks. I'm sorry to spring this on you but it was time. When you didn't show up these last couple of days, I worried that I'd messed up and might not have a chance to explain myself or my actions."

"Desperate times."

"I swear this was my idea. I thought that if the kids met away from any pressure to get along or accept each other, it would be easier for them."

"I agree. It's been good for them to make new friends, apart from your relationship with Eva. More natural than forcing them together." He watched as the children climbed off the play equipment and started a game of tag as they wove their way toward the bench and the waiting men.

"I'll think on this," Bernie promised. "I'm not happy that you saw fit to bamboozle me, but your heart's in the right place." Disappointment filled his gaze. "If I were a younger man, you'd be on the ground for messing with me like this."

"Yes, sir. And you'd be right."

Bernie sighed. "But, with Estelle on a crutch, and the kids growing like weeds, needing more from us, I see our daily lives differently than I did three days ago. And I admit to feeling guilty about what we did to Eva."

It was too early to be relieved. He asked cautiously, "You'll talk to Estelle?"

Bernie grunted assent. "She may be more amenable since she's feeling her age right now. But I'll have to take time to figure out how best to approach her." Bernie cleared his throat. "To be clear, what is it you hope for out of this?"

Jesse considered before he responded. "I want Eva to have free access to her children. For myself? I want Eva and her children in my life. I want my children to accept hers as permanent." It was a stretch, but in a perfect world, he'd get everything he dreamed of. "I'm pretty sure Eva wants me, too, but we haven't spoken for three days. She's convinced my kids won't accept hers."

"She knows they're already friends."

"Yes. But according to Farren, a mutual friend, Eva's convinced we have no future together and she wants a clean break for my sake."

The children arrived like a murder of crows looking for food, heads tilting, eyes glued to the cooler bag filled with snacks that Bernie was unzipping. "Here you go," he said as he handed out brownies and juice boxes.

Jesse sent Eva a text. "Bernie knows about us. Please talk to me."

Chapter Eighteen

"Bernie knows about us. Please talk to me." Eva read Jesse's latest text. She stared at it for twenty minutes, at least—no, it only *felt* like minutes had ticked by—thirty seconds, tops. Still, the words were loaded, frightening, and for those long, long, seconds she wasn't sure what to do.

Talk to him.

She abandoned her book and set it on the table beside her reading chair. The words hadn't made sense anyway, not with the way her mind had skipped around. Basically, she'd ignored Jesse's messages for three days. But this one, she had to deal with.

She stared at the words again and mulled all they could mean.

Bernie must be furious about Jesse's manipulation. Estelle had probably heard already. They could have talked to a lawyer already.

Anger rose from her churning belly. Jesse had ruined her already-precarious life by butting in, by asking her to trust that he could befriend Bernie and influence him to support Eva. How had Bernie found out? Had Jesse confessed? She cringed inside and flexed her hands into fists.

This was her fault. Again. After all she'd learned from Rhys, why had she gone along with another man's decision? Because she was desperate, despairing of her children ever being with her.

And suddenly, her anger with Jesse dissipated like fog touched by the sun's rays.

Ultimately, the blame for this mess was on her. She should have talked Jesse out of this scheme of his. Shouldn't have trusted that he understood the mystery of how men think. A part of her had doubted the plan would work, but she'd ignored her smarter self because she'd wanted to hold onto her dream.

Dreams could crush a person. She should have known better than to trust that Jesse could deliver hers on a platter. *Foolish woman. Look what you've done now.* She should have known dreams were for fools.

Trust of a man had been the reason she lost her kids in the first place. She'd trusted Rhys when he said she didn't need to adopt the girls. She hadn't pushed because their father knew best. That's what her mom had always said, and Eva had believed it.

She'd had niggles about seeing to the legalities, but after a while, she'd ignored her inner voice and gone along for the sake of harmony. She'd had years of a happy, suburban life, with a great job, a loving husband, beautiful daughters.

Maybe she hadn't wanted to do or say anything to rock the boat, to force Rhys into doing something he didn't want to do. Whenever she'd broached the subject of adoption, he'd deflected.

He'd hidden the existence of the custody agreement from her because he didn't want to argue with her or explain. She'd known Rhys didn't like confrontation and they rarely had a cross word between them, but she should've insisted.

Now, here she was, faced with more fallout because of her poor choices. She needed to step up and insist on having access to the girls. Now, before Estelle won their hearts and Eva became nothing but a memory with no more relevance than a childhood pet.

No. She couldn't let that happen. Acting now was her best option. She stood and went to the bathroom to splash water on her face. Her reflection in the mirror over the sink showed a woman with nerves of steel and an unbendable will. The smile she gave herself was cold, icy with determination. If Jesse had told Bernie the truth, then it was time she took on the bear.

Stepping up meant facing Estelle, woman to woman. She ran a comb through her hair, brushed her teeth and then glared at her reflection for a moment longer.

Eva allowed a grim smile of anticipation to settle on her lips.

But first she needed to put Jesse out of his misery. She texted him back. "Come over tonight. We'll talk." He'd never been to her home, just the daycare. One more text and then she'd leave. "Rook's Nest Cottage." She hit send and contained a flutter of nerves.

THE DOOR OPENED AND there she was. Estelle, her years-long nemesis. The woman behind the decisions that had taken Eva's children from her. She'd aged since Eva had last seen her only months ago. She gave the older woman a long, slow, up and down look. "I'm here to talk about my daughters." Her tone was flat, hard. Insistent.

Estelle's eyes widened at first glance as shock filled her face. "This is unacceptable. You can't show up uninvited and without an appointment."

Eva shook her head. "No. What is unacceptable is you tearing my girls away from the only mom they've known. They've lost enough, Estelle." She raised her chin and stared into wide, faded blue eyes. "No more."

Her vibrancy was gone. It wasn't just her eyes that had faded. The woman looked exhausted with dark circles under her eyes and her skin had lost color. Rhys's mother-in-law had been a vital, active woman with tons of energy. But this woman looked defeated, and old beyond her years. Raising two active girls could wear on a woman. But this looked like more than a lost night's sleep.

"Are you all right?" Eva blurted. "What's going on? Is it Bernie? Has something happened?" Her mind raced while she watched Estelle consider her next words. But Eva wouldn't leave without making her point. She prepared to stand in the doorway for as long as it took. "I won't leave until you tell me."

"You should come in," Estelle opened the door wider, revealing a crutch and a wrapped ankle. "I can't stand for long." She hopped backward to give Eva room to enter.

Surprised with the injury, Eva stepped inside. "Did you break it?"

"A bad sprain when I—." She abruptly cut off her words.

"You don't have to tell me about it," Eva said as she closed the door. At least now she knew the reason for the sudden change in Estelle's appearance. Pain and crutches could knock the wind out of anyone. "Not my business and I'm not here for a friendly chat."

"Of course you're not." Estelle hobbled awkwardly toward the expansive living room. Formal, the furniture looked as if no one sat there. Ever. "You'll forgive me if I don't offer refreshments."

"Naturally." She waited until Estelle had chosen a seat. That it was nearest the entryway, meant she was in real discomfort. It must burn to appear anything but perfect.

Estelle sat stiffly at the edge of the firm sofa and rested her crutch within easy reach. Her hand slid toward her bandaged ankle, but she stopped before she touched it.

Show no weakness must be her motto, Eva thought.

"Would you like a cushion at your back?" Eva lifted one and Estelle leaned forward to accommodate the support. After she placed the cushion, Eva perched in a wing chair kitty corner to the sofa. She did not lean back but stayed on the edge with her shoulders squared and her backbone straight.

"Thank you. Bernie has the girls at the play park. Something about a pond with frogs and a tribe of children who hunt for them. Now that the girls can swim, I allowed their participation Apparently, there's a young boy they're taken with. They missed going for a couple of days and I was afraid of all-out mutiny."

"I can't see you accepting mutiny," Eva said in a dry tone.

Estelle hmphed.

Tyler. Raine. Thea. That's why Jesse had texted. He'd come clean at the park today and Estelle was still unaware of Jesse's admission.

Tyler could charm anyone and the idea of him playing with her children made her smile. "New friends? I'm glad. And a pond with frogs? Jilly loves the natural world. Rhys encouraged her. He'd be proud she kept up her interest."

Warmth flashed behind the other woman's eyes. "Yes, he would. Rhys was a good father."

"The best." Eva nodded. "And he was a loving husband. A kind man." Eva fidgeted with the seam of her jeans. "He was kind to you when you lost your daughter. He signed the custody agreement you wanted to ease your grief. I understand that. I've tried hard to forgive him for not telling me about it."

Estelle bit her lip and had the grace to flush. But she said nothing.

Eva continued. "After we married, I asked to adopt the girls, but he put me off. I suspect you knew that I was never told about the agreement. Maybe you're the one who convinced him to keep it secret. That wouldn't have been hard. Rhys wouldn't have wanted to hurt you, so he'd have gone along with whatever you wanted."

Again, silence. She sighed and nodded. "If I'd pressed him more, forced the issue, *if I'd stood up for myself,* we wouldn't be in this predicament now. I wouldn't still be angry with Rhys."

Estelle pursed her lips. "Where might we be then? In your opinion what would've happened if Rhys had allowed the adoption?"

She'd had a lot of time to ponder the what ifs and hows of her life if she still had the girls. "I'd have stayed at my job, kept my home, and you'd have continued to see Sophie and Jilly as you'd always done."

A small huff of air. "Come now, you expect me to believe you wouldn't have married again? Been looking for your next husband right away?" She worried her lip and then gave a nonchalant shrug. "Most women would have been happy to be free of stepchildren so they could move on." She waved a hand as if disposing of children was akin to a donation to a thrift store.

"But that's not what I did, is it? After Rhys died, you misjudged me the way you always did. You decided I was a desperate woman looking to grab onto a man, any man, just to be married." She shook her head. "I need to say it wasn't Rhys who I fell for first. It was your beautiful granddaughters. They needed me, Estelle. They needed my love and commitment, and I gave them my all. Rhys was the bonus."

Estelle blinked several times as she took in Eva's words. They'd never spoken this way before; as women who loved deeply and wanted the best for two girls who deserved to have all the love they could need.

"Sophie and Jilly still need me," she said, her voice breaking. "Still love me and clearly, I love them. I believe I've shown you how much by moving to Last Chance Beach." She leaned forward to help press her point. "In your heart, you know it's true."

Estelle's face blanked. But a blank face wasn't a denial and Eva took the advantage. "I'm a short drive away, have a daycare opening in two weeks. What more can I do to show you that I'm their mom and I love them like any other mother. As much as your daughter did." She settled fully into the chair. "Because of that love, I would never keep them from you. I've lived too long without them to do the same to you."

"Not even now? Not after what we did?" Her gaze hit the floor and she shifted, looking uncomfortable. At last.

"Not even now," Eva vowed softly. "I used to believe I wanted full custody. A sort of revenge, but no more."

Estelle's brows knit. "What then?"

"Sharing them is the better choice. They love you. Their aunt and uncle are in Summerville. I'm right over the bridge. Their school is here and I'm sure it's the best in the county, because you'd make certain of that."

Estelle nodded. "Of course."

"We could share them. There will be times you'll need backup. All caregivers do. Let me be part of their lives. We'll all be happier, including you and Bernie." Eva had a thought. "Have you decided when the girls will be old enough to have their own phones?" Sophie had mentioned that her friends were starting to get them.

"They're too young."

"They're not too young to be prepared for online safety. Sophie especially. I've already looked into software that will help protect them online. I'd make sure you understand how it works."

Estelle shifted and looked uncomfortable with the turn in the discussion. Time to change the subject and turn the screw tighter. "How did you hurt your ankle?"

"It was a fall. Nothing much." One shoulder lifted and fell. "I'm fine. Bernie's fine and helped with the girls and household chores. He tried, but he's not much of a cook."

The way Estelle had of offering a compliment and a complaint in the same breath hadn't changed. "I'm sure he did all he could. He's a good man. A good grandfather." Eva let a beat go by. "But a fall could've been much more serious."

Estelle nodded. "I've thought of little else."

"The girls are already busy, and their lives will only get busier. Sophie is social and when she hits middle school, she'll be in lots of activities. You'll be driving them around constantly. Sports, friends, shopping."

"Apparently with their faces stuck in their phones." Estelle cocked an eyebrow in an echo of the fierce woman Eva had seen in her kitchen on the day of Rhys's funeral.

Eva shrugged. "Technology is the way of the world today. We must accept it, learn how to control it or our children can be run over."

"My son has mentioned phones. I can have him explain what I'll need to do."

"Of course." But it was clear she'd made the older woman think twice. She nodded as if she'd said her piece.

Estelle gave her a sharp glance. "I'm glad you came by," she said stiffly, dismissively. "You've given me much to ponder, Eva. I'll discuss this visit with our son, his wife, and Bernie." She looked at her watch, a step counter, because Estelle was usually quite active. "But they'll be home soon and..." she trailed off.

Eva understood. This visit hadn't been planned. "The girls should be prepared ahead of time for a visit from me. They need to know that we're talking, though. Can you do that, please? Tell them I came by and that there will be some changes?"

"After I think and *after* I discuss things with the family."

"Good. I'm glad." Eva already knew that Estelle's son and his wife had been on her side. They probably still were. They'd got along well whenever they'd been together. She and Rhys had flown from California to Summerville at different times for family events. Eva would leave the house more confident than when she'd arrived. "No need to walk me out. You rest. The girls will be whirlwinds when they come home."

Estelle nodded.

Eva rose and crossed to the other woman, set her fingertips to her shoulder. "Estelle," she said. "Thank you for this. I realize it wasn't easy." She hoped that Bernie was being as thoughtful with whatever Jesse had admitted.

Estelle nodded and patted Eva's fingers where they lay.

By the time Eva got to her scooter, she decided the dampness she'd seen in the other woman's eyes was a trick of the light.

But maybe, Estelle had been doing some re-evaluating or soul-searching lately. It couldn't be easy with two active girls in her home at her age. Eva wanted to believe that the sprained ankle and crutches had forced the older woman to consider what could happen if her health was suddenly compromised.

Chapter Nineteen

Three days of silence. Three. Jesse smoothed his hair and felt sweat break out on the back of his neck as he waited for Eva to answer her door. He'd driven straight over from Summerville Park after his talk with Bernie, stopping only to leave his kids with Sal and Tina.

All he wanted was to see Eva, talk to her, and most importantly, convince her to forgive him. This was his chance to find a solution to what Eva saw as a monumental problem, but what Jesse believed to be a minor roadblock.

The door opened.

His breath caught at first sight of her. A man devoid of water drank deeply at his first chance, and his eyes were no different. He drank her in. Her hair was tousled, half dry from a shower. Perfect. In a blink, he started to talk.

"Hi," he blurted. "I'm sure we can get the girls to come around. They're already friends with Sophie and Jilly. This isn't as bad as it looks, and I'm sure there's a way around it." The words shot out of his mouth, desperate and pathetic. But Eva, brave, wonderful Eva looked ready to cry. He opened his arms.

She walked into them. *Thank God, she walked into them.*

He shuddered as he enveloped her and held her tight. She released a sigh that went right through him. Eva tucked her head near his shoulder and let him hold on as tight as he needed to. Because he *needed* to. "I expected you'd tell me to leave, that you'd blame me if Estelle didn't listen to Bernie."

Kids rode by on bikes, and he heard their chatter and laughter as it faded into the distance. He wasn't sure, but they may have been laughing at the couple clinging to each other in the doorway of Rook's Nest Cottage. "May I come in?"

"Oh! Yes, of course." Eva backed up but held him by the forearms, so he'd follow. Her face flushed pink. "I'm happy to see you," she admitted with a tremulous smile. "I'm sorry I ghosted you. I shouldn't have."

"Does three days count as ghosting?"

"It felt like a lifetime." She continued her reverse course into the narrow hallway, keeping a firm grip on his arms. He allowed her to tow him because it was clear she wasn't about to let him go.

Jesse kicked the door shut behind him and then they had all the privacy in the world. "We need to talk," he said, when he wanted to do anything but. "I may have made a worse mess of things today and I need to explain."

She shook her head. "I probably ruined all the good you did, anyway." She groaned and then admitted, "I faced off with Estelle."

Stunned, he froze as he processed her words. "Oh. Wow. You did?" She nodded.

At that he said, "I need a drink." She must've raced over to face Estelle right after his text about Bernie. He dreaded to hear what happened. But she'd fallen into his arms, so how bad could it be?

"Beer's in the fridge. Take a seat and I'll be right back."

He hadn't been inside her home before. Curious, he took stock. She had a new-looking sofa and overstuffed chair, with a floor lamp beside it aimed at the seat. He imagined her reading in that chair, legs curled to the side as the light cascaded over her shoulder. The floor sported a classic area rug, and from where he stood, he could see through to the kitchen. She'd splurged on brand new appliances, as well.

Eva had put her stamp on the place to make it homey and welcoming. The paint looked fresh with up-to-date muted tones. The cottage was cozily decorated, with furniture that cried out to be relaxed into. Eva's home was all that welcomed warmth and good times. Family pictures adorned the mantel over the small gas fireplace. It looked new, too, but her choice of surround and mantel matched with the age of the house. Had she had it installed?

She'd kept the original charm and character of her home. He wouldn't be surprised to learn that she'd tackled most of the work on her own.

He checked out the pictures on the mantel. A man he assumed was Rhys held a newborn baby in two separate photos. Eva had honored her husband's life from before she'd joined his family. She also displayed a full family studio style portrait of Rhys, his first wife, and Sophie, about two, and Jilly, in her mom's arms.

The family photo was sweet and familiar because Jesse had a similar portrait. An image of him with Lynne and the three children graced the wall in the dining room of his home.

"Here you go," Eva said as she handed him an ice-cold beer in a pilsener glass. "They were a happy, loving family," she said as she stood beside him. She touched a fingertip to the family portrait. "Rhys often talked with Sophie and Jilly about that time in their lives. He wanted them to have a sense of their mother's love. The girls know how loving their family was." She drew in a shaky breath. "How much they were loved by their parents."

"Still *are* loved."

She flashed him a grateful smile and a glance. "Yes. That's true."

"You never wanted to usurp her place." He set the glass on a coaster on the coffee table.

"I don't believe another woman can take a mother's place, not completely. But there can be two loves in a life, even in a child's."

He swallowed as her words hit home. "You loved Rhys and I loved Lynne."

She turned and looked up into his gaze, her eyes watchful. "Yes," she said carefully.

"And now," he replied, "I love you." All the pieces fell into place. The reason he'd stuck his nose into her business and maneuvered his way into a friendship with Bernie, how he'd made it easy for his children to meet her without pressure.

"I love you, too. And your kids." A cloud crossed her face. She chewed her lip, drawing his gaze to her mouth. Her oh-so-kissable mouth. "I didn't want to fall in love." She flushed. "You understand that first night we were together was about forgetting. About oblivion. You gave me what I wanted but I denied wanting more."

He nodded. "Been there myself."

"I've been down this road once. I fell for a single dad, a good man. I've lost more than I can bear, but I love you and that's just the way it is." Her shrug made her seem small and vulnerable, but not weak. Eva Fontaine would never be weak. Could never be weak.

He took her glass from her hand, and not taking his eyes from hers, set it beside his on the coffee table. He could drown in her and be happy.

Jesse gathered her close and kissed her. Kissed her gently. Kissed her firmly. Kissed her the way a man does when the woman in his arms holds his heart. Her tongue sought his and resolutely he offered his own and much more. He offered Eva all that he was. She fit him. Fit his life, fit in his arms, fit with his children. They'd be happy with Eva in their lives, and he knew it in every bit of muscle and sinew.

After more than a few long, slow kisses that raised his temperature, he raised his head. "We're in this together, Eva. No more days of not responding. No more hiding from me or from our future together."

"Right. I'm sorry I ignored your texts and calls. It was hell for me, too." Her eyes filled with tears. "I panicked when Raine said they'd accept me, but not my daughters. It was a wild high when they approved of me and just as quickly, it turned into the lowest low. How did we miss telling them I'm a package deal?"

"Easy. We focused on them getting to know you gradually, making it easy to like you. Singles' Fest is a no pressure thing, but we went the extra. And don't forget, they were already making friends with Sophie and Jilly at the park. We wanted that relationship to have time to grow, too."

"I hope we handled things okay." She shook her head, clearly distressed. "So much can go wrong. We're in a minefield."

He looped his hands behind her waist and rocked from side to side, like middle-schoolers in a slow dance. "We did what we thought was best. It was different from what most dating parents do, but given our circumstances, it made sense."

"You've given this a lot of consideration."

"How did you and Rhys handle dating at first? How long before you met his daughters?"

Her gaze shifted inward. A soft smile played on her lips as she pulled up memories. "We dated for a month before he asked me to meet them. We decided to take them for a walk along the boardwalk at Mission Beach. Getting them and their strollers out of the SUV needed more than one person. He handed Jilly to me to hold, and with one look into her sweet face, I fell in love. He pulled out the strollers and when he finished setting them up, he looked at me and gave me this lopsided smile and I could tell he'd seen the love on my face. From there, the decisions came quickly." She sighed. "But Sophie and Jilly were very young and accepted me right away."

"It's different when they're old enough to express opinions."

"We can't force your daughters to change their minds. To attempt it would make family life miserable. I can imagine how vocal my girls are with Estelle and Bernie."

"Let's not get on the guilt train, here, Eva. Maybe we could have worked you being a single mom into the conversations but then we'd have been explaining Estelle and Bernie to them, too. Who knows what they'd think if they heard that grandparents could take kids away from a mom who loves them? Your situation was too complicated for children to sort out."

She frowned and mulled over what he'd said. "Okay, now I feel better."

"We need to discuss how my talk with Bernie went today." He kissed her softly as it dawned on him that he'd far exceeded his hope for this meeting. *Eva Fontaine loved him and his kids.* He let the realization flow through his body. "Although I'd much rather spend more time kissing you. It just came to me that we're totally alone here, with no children waiting for us."

She snuggled close. "Please spend the night, Jesse. It's been a long time since that first night and it's Friday. We can have the day together tomorrow, too as long as your in-laws are okay keeping Raine, Thea and Tyler."

"Sal and Tina know I'm here, trying to salvage what we have. I've told them what happened. Then let's talk through whatever we both have to say. Afterward, we can set it aside and focus on us. Just us. For once." *And for the whole night.* His heartrate picked up and blood rushed to all the good places.

"Agreed." She chuckled as her eyes danced with a light he rarely saw when talk turned to her former in-laws. The light spelled mischief and he loved that she looked happy and glowing. "You should've seen Estelle's face when she opened the door and saw me. I must have given off a 'don't mess with me' vibe because she let me in, pretty as you please."

She led him to sit on the sofa. Facing each other, knees touching, she began. "Estelle promised to talk with the family about my visit. She said she'd consider regular visits with the girls if that was the consensus from her son and his wife and Bernie."

"Bernie told me Estelle's severely sprained ankle was a wake-up call. Let's hope that's true. Did she use her crutch?"

She nodded. "But she declined to say how it happened."

"Carrying a loaded laundry basket down the stairs to the basement."

"She *fell*?" Her eyes went wide. "And all that happened was a sprained ankle?"

He nodded. "When Bernie saw her at the foot of the stairs, he had a helluva fright."

EVA ROSE, TRIED TO wrap her head around the what ifs that bounced around in her mind. She picked up their forgotten beer glasses and handed his to Jesse, who gratefully accepted and took a sip. She did, too.

"Will this be enough to have them soften toward me?" Estelle had been different with her. "She wasn't what I'd call warm, but her usual chill wasn't there, either."

If she'd known how Estelle had injured her ankle when she'd been there, she could've said more.

"Yes, I believe they'll soften. Bernie said their son and his wife were firmly on your side in this. They've been louder about it since that incident when they caught their boys bullying the girls. They feel that the boys wouldn't have said what they did if you were around more. They say that when the boys saw their grandparents take the girls from you, they were triggered into saying things they shouldn't."

"They used to tease the girls about living with an evil stepmother." Rhys refused to talk to the girls' aunt and uncle about it, though. Again, he viewed a conversation about their boys comments as confrontational. And again, she'd accepted her husband's decision and had done what she could to be friendly with her nephews.

"That's rough." He dropped an arm across her shoulder, drew her close and kissed her temple. She loved him for it. Jesse was comfort and strength and love in one sexy body. "If you want to talk with them face-to-face, I'll go with you."

She wasn't sure if that was the best course of action. "Maybe we've had enough face-to-face for now. Both Estelle and Bernie have been offered our thoughts today. We might do better to let the family discuss things privately."

Jesse frowned but nodded his assent. "I want to put an end to this, but I'll respect your wishes. We'll give them time and hope for the best, most reasonable solution."

She saw it then. A huge difference between Jesse and Rhys was Jesse's ability to handle difficult conversations. He'd taken charge when he decided to meet Bernie in the park for the first time. He'd faced off with the older man today and had set things in motion that could lead to a rational reality for everyone involved. And then, he'd backed off immediately when she asked him to.

Light and warmth filled her as she gazed at him, this man who loved and listened to her.

"Do you know what I'm proud of?" Jesse said, breaking into her thoughts.

"No. What?"

"The way you marched over to confront Estelle. Once I said Bernie knew about us and how I'd maneuvered things with him, you didn't back down or hide or let the men handle it. You took the reins and faced your worst tormentor."

She snorted. "I let a man handle the most important thing in my life once and I lost." But this wasn't about Rhys anymore. She let him go. She released her disappointment in him and in herself.

Today was about her future with this man, Jesse Carmichael, and his kids. And *her* kids. "I was scared on the way to see her, because Estelle is fearsome and has kept her whole family in line through this past year. They tiptoe around her, and I understand why. Losing her daughter and then her son-in-law was more than she could stand. As a result, she clung to Sophie and Jilly. It's only human. But I should've faced her sooner."

She'd been close to tears whenever she'd seen Estelle in California. During her challenge of the custody agreement, she'd been close to hysterical with grief after losing Rhys. She'd battled terror at the thought of losing Sophie and Jilly. It had been a hard eight months with the move across the country, the decision to open *NanaBanana*, and the slow gains she'd made with seeing the girls. Even the video chats had only happened for a handful of weeks. And they'd occurred only because of Bernie's soft heart.

So much of the last year had been out of her control, that she'd been overwhelmed at the idea of facing down Estelle. But she had faced her, and Jesse was proud of her and even more, she was proud of herself.

That pride let her reach for Jesse, in a way that spelled fulfillment and love. "Jesse, make love to me. Be my love, my life, mine, to have and hold from this day forward."

The room swooped, tilted, and swirled as Jesse lifted her into his arms and froze. "Are you sure?" he asked, looking hopeful but careful at the same time. "Because this time will mean more than the last time."

Chapter Twenty

"I want you," Eva assured Jesse between kisses. She fisted his shirtfront to keep from falling out of his arms. "Be with me tonight. There's nothing I want more." He held her up, his face mere inches away from hers. His eyes gleamed with banked desire, and she was certain he'd drop her as soon as he realized she wasn't a featherweight, which would be any moment now. But Jesse held her steadily, with no sign of strain.

"Which way to your room?" The man didn't even labor to breathe.

"Down the hall, last door on the left." The room was modest, like all the rooms in Rook's Nest Cottage, but the bed was new, comfortable, and empty without him. "Stay the night," she murmured against his neck. Then she licked his skin there and a shudder ran through him. Delighted with his response, she licked his ear next, then drew his lobe between her lips.

"That's not fair. I'm busy here," he teased with a deep smile. "Yes, I'll stay the night. There's nothing that could make me happier." He stopped outside her bedroom door and looked into her eyes. "I told Sal and Tina I may not be home tonight, and they should keep the children. They didn't ask why, but Sal slapped me on the back and Tina kissed my cheek."

"Were you that sure of your reception from me?" It was sweet that he'd share his in-laws' reactions. They sounded like good people. She'd meet them someday soon. Surely, there would never be another Estelle in her life. *Hm.*

"Sure of *you*? Not at all. I only hoped you'd allow us to date." He grinned. "If you'd turned me away, my plan was to sit at The Sandbar and drown my sorrows before stumbling to a room and falling face first into an empty bed."

She chuckled at the image. She still had a question, though. "You promise Sal and Tina will accept me?"

"I do. They're warm and kind and I've promised they'll always have the children in their lives." His assurance eased her mind.

"They will," she vowed. "When I meet them, I'll promise them, too." She let her thoughts slip away while her body took over. Yearning, desire, and love spun through her like kites over the ocean. "As to our dating. We've been on how many dates? Three? Four? That's enough to feel right." And it was so right she wanted to shout with joy. Life had allowed lightning to strike twice, and she reveled in it.

"It's enough time for me," he chuffed and moved into the room. As he held her over the bed, he continued, "I was halfway in love with you when we first met in The Sandbar and Archie talked you into letting us sit with you and Farren."

"You looked interested in the business items we talked about. You answered Farren's relationship questions. An interested man is hard to resist." Thrills ran through her at the memory. They'd come far since that day.

He snorted. "I remember every word you said that day, and maybe each one since."

"Okay, now you're fishing."

"A little. Is it working?"

"Oh, yes," she whispered against his lips.

He set her on the bed and followed her down.

THE NEXT MORNING, JESSE woke to a chime coming from somewhere nearby. Groggy, he rolled over and peeped an eye open. Eva faced him, still asleep. He raised his head to find the source of the chime. Her phone. It was the sound of a video call. "Eva. Eva, wake up, sweetheart." He touched her shoulder lightly.

"Huh? What?" She bolted to a sit and swiped hair out of her eyes, looking tousled and well-loved. A flash of pride rolled through him when he realized they'd have many more mornings when she'd look like this; happy, satisfied, and joyful. She smiled and blew him a kiss before she lifted her phone. She glanced at the screen then turned to him wide-eyed with surprise. "It's the girls! Stay still and don't say a word."

When he settled out of range of the camera, she tapped her screen to accept the video call. "Hi, good morning," she said, her voice full of sleep and welcome. "What's going on?"

"Mom! Guess what?" Sophie squealed. Jesse recognized her voice because he'd heard that squeal plenty of times in the park. He smiled but made sure to stay out of view.

"She won't guess. Tell her, silly," Jilly demanded. Their heads touched as their faces filled the screen.

"Okay. Gramma says we can see you today! We're coming over to your house, right now!"

"Now?" She tossed him a sidelong glance. He slid out of the bed as stealthily as he could.

Another woman's voice came through the phone. "Unless it's a bad time?"

"Of course not, Estelle." She swiped at her hair again, but Jesse thought it was a lost cause. Her eyes darted as her mind raced. Eva was still half-asleep, and her life had taken a sudden, sharp turn. "I'll put coffee on. I don't know about you, but I need some." She frowned. "Have the girls had breakfast?"

Out of sight of the camera, she waved at him to hurry. He gathered his jeans, socks, and underwear, but his shirt had been tossed out of sight. He looked under the bed and found it as the women continued planning. He had an hour before Eva's company arrived. No doubt they'd have a lot to discuss, but he didn't have the right yet to stay and support her through this.

Unless he was invited to stay, he needed to leave. Pronto.

Feeling like a teenager caught in his girlfriend's room, he threw on his clothes and hit the bathroom. When he exited a few minutes later, he found Eva waiting for her turn.

"I want to stay with you," he said. "But I understand if you need to do this alone."

"Exposing us,"—she waved her hand between their bodies— "to the girls might be too much at once," she said with regret. "I haven't said I'm dating anyone, let alone you. I'll tell them today. Bernie will be here, as well. That will help."

"By now, he's told Estelle about me. I bet you'll see how she's leaning immediately."

"She looked resigned when we chatted. Maybe in person, she'll warm up." Eva shrugged.

"I hope so." He drew her into his arms. "This isn't how I pictured our first morning together."

"Me, either." She raised her face for his kiss, and they clung together for a long moment. "But having my kids here is more than I could've imagined a couple of days ago. I'm happy enough to burst."

He kissed her one last time for luck. "Call me. I'm hanging around for a long walk on the beach until I hear from you."

EVA LOVED THAT JESSE didn't go far when he left the cottage. Coffee started, she showered, straightened the bedroom, and then headed into the living room to dust and tidy. Her kitchen had been cleaned before Jesse had arrived yesterday. She checked the time, ignoring the butterflies she felt in her belly. She'd never been this nervous in her life. Not when she met the people in Rhys's life, not on her wedding day, not ever.

She got coffee mugs out, along with cream and sugar and mentally prepared for the meeting. When she'd first met Estelle and Bernie, Estelle had been cool and distant, her expression dismissive. Naturally, she'd assumed that over time, the older woman would warm to her. Eva had done her best to be friendly with and understand Estelle. Despite her efforts cold distance had become entrenched between them. Bernie had been kind and awkward at their first meeting and that hadn't changed either.

She pulled out the girls' favorite juice from her pantry and set it in the chill drawer of her fridge so that the small boxes would be cool when they arrived.

Her daughters were coming to see her. Here. In her cottage in Last Chance Beach, only thirty minutes from where they lived.

She stopped with her hand on the fridge door and felt a sob rush up from her soul into her heart. Eva sniffled. *Get it together.*

The doorbell chimed, cheery and expectant with the promise of visitors she wanted to welcome with open arms. As she hurried to the door, she dashed tears from her cheeks, but she'd run out of time to collect her emotions. Besides, her shields were down so she could feel the love from her children.

Sophie and Jilly pushed inside immediately, and she gathered them close, tears falling again. Through her watery gaze, she caught a look between Estelle and Bernie, as they waited on the front porch. Dare she hope it was a look of contrition?

The girls were as overcome as she was, their words drowned by sobs and relief. "Mom. Mommy. Mom." She could barely make out the words, but they were the sweetest she'd ever heard. She hadn't held them in months, hadn't sniffed their hair or pressed her lips to their foreheads. But she could do it now, so she did it all several times.

An hour later, she sat on the sofa wedged between Sophie and Jilly. She'd given her guests a tour of her home, had served drinks, and barely kept from squeezing the life out of her daughters.

Estelle sat in the comfy chair that Eva used for reading, while Bernie had brought in a dining room chair to sit on.

"Rook's Nest Cottage is small," Eva said, as she looked from Sophie to Jilly. "But the girls have the larger of the two bedrooms since they need twin beds, and I don't need the space they do." They'd already established that the girls would spend the night at least once a month. Eva had been giddy when Bernie made the suggestion and Estelle had agreed.

"It's cozy," Estelle said with an approving look. "I imagine you invested heavily in the daycare you're opening."

Jilly piped up. "NanaBanana."

Her grandmother smiled at her with a nod. "Thank you, Jillian."

"That's right," Eva said to Estelle. "I weighed my needs for living against my need to *make* a living and when I found this place, it felt right. Perfect." She'd sold her furniture in California, not wanting to be reminded of her old life. And when she got here, the rooms were smaller than expected. Virtual tours were great, but size could be distorted. She'd had to choose her furniture carefully.

Thankfully, her nerves weren't as rattled now that they'd settled in the living room and conversation felt more normal in its ebb and flow. Her heart beat at its normal rate for the first time since she got their call earlier.

"Our first house was a fixer upper, remember Bernie?" She slanted her husband an affectionate glance that made Eva blink in surprise.

Flags of red appeared on his cheekbones. "I exaggerated my handyman abilities to impress my bride." He sat with his elbows on his knees, relaxed.

Estelle rolled her eyes. "It cost a fortune to fix whatever he broke, and he broke whatever he attempted to fix." She patted his knee. "But when you're young you can live with mistakes. Accept them." She eyed Eva kindly which made her straighten. "I hope that you can accept that we—that I—made several mistakes with you over the years. It seems each one built on the ones before." She shifted and she pursed her lips. "Can you forgive me?"

Sophie jerked as if she'd been struck. Eva slipped her arm around the girl's shoulders. "Yes," her daughter answered for her, "yes, she can if it means we can have her back now."

Estelle's gaze shifted to Sophie. "Are you saying one weekend a month isn't enough?"

"It's not, Jilly and I want more. Don't we, Jilly?"

Jilly nodded, wide-eyed and dumbfounded.

"I want us to move forward and put this horrible year behind us," Eva added. "I can move to Summerville and keep my daycare here. There's a need on the island. Employment growth demands it. I can rent this place out to visitors if I move to Summerville. There's brisk business in short term rental on the island." She hoped not to have to move again, but she'd do whatever it took. Jesse would support her decision and her faith in him eased her mind.

Wherever she lived, whatever happened with Jesse, she had her children back in her life.

Her dream had come true and with Jesse, the impossible had happened. She'd found love again. She held her secret to her heart and hugged her girls one more time in celebration.

Bernie suddenly made a show of checking his watch and then cleared his throat. "I believe it's time for us to leave, Estelle. Eva will be taking the girls out soon."

"I will?" She hadn't known they'd be here at all, and now plans for an outing had been made for her. "What's happening?" she asked curiously, glad that Jesse hadn't gone far. Maybe they could catch up to him on the beach.

Estelle rose, slipped her single crutch under her shoulder, and said, "Girls, you may stay with your mother for the rest of the day. We'll pick you up later. I'd like to check out the changes in Last Chance Beach. We haven't been here in years."

Bernie smiled, a mischievous light in his eyes. "We assumed you'd want to show the girls The Landseer Motel. I hear the pool's full of children and the playground's lots of fun."

Estelle hobbled toward the front door. "Bernie will bring in a bag with their bathing suits and towels. He also brought my brownies that he's apparently famous for."

Famous brownies and the motel pool? This conversation had taken a curious turn, but clearly, the turn was in Eva's favor, and she filled with gratitude.

Eva went to the other woman's side. "Estelle," she said on a deep breath. "Thank you."

"I've let go of many resentments, and a great deal of anger around losing my daughter. I'm sorry I took this long, Eva." Estelle drew her in for a light hug.

Eva's heart pinched as she felt the other woman's deep grief. "I always understood," she said next to Estelle's ear. She stepped back, clasped Estelle's forearms lightly and said, "I believed we'd work things out with Rhys's help."

"I probably hoped for the same thing, but losing him, too—it knocked the stuffing out of me."

Eva kissed Estelle's cheek. "You were afraid you'd lose the girls." A look passed between them that Eva never expected. A look full of emotion and understanding. A look that massaged the hurt parts of her soul. She blinked slowly to absorb the change that had come to them.

"It took time to accept that I needed help," Estelle explained, "but I finally attended grief counseling after we moved here. When I fell down the stairs, and had to re-evaluate my abilities, I did the hard work I needed to do. I had a *lot* to work out." She patted Eva's shoulder. "For too long, I blamed you. I have no idea why, except that I needed to direct my anger somewhere. Counselling helped more than I expected."

Eva nodded, appreciating her honesty. "We'll move forward from here. I promise."

The other woman gave her a wan but encouraging smile. "I've been told you keep your promises." She stepped out onto the porch and turned back to face Eva. "There's still work for me to do, but I believe I've turned a corner. I hope you believe that."

Bernie returned from the car with a beach bag full of gear for the girls. Inside, were swimsuits she hadn't bought for them, beach towels she'd never seen. Proof of the time they'd been apart and of how they'd grown since she'd had them with her. She gave her head a small shake, clearing her leftover outrage to make room for hope. Hope that her life was about to change for the better.

Her better future included Jesse Carmichael and his three boisterous children. She set aside her nerves about Raine and Thea. They'd come around. Because love had a way of smoothing rough edges so that hope could blossom.

A thrill grew from her belly. *Jesse.* He hadn't gone for a walk on the beach, after all. He'd picked up his children and he waited with them at the motel. His family waited for hers to join them.

He wanted to come clean. She gathered her nerve and felt Sophie and Jilly flank her. Jilly's hand slipped into hers, as if the child felt the change coming.

"Bernie?"

He clasped her hand in both of his, gave her fingers a squeeze.

"You'll work things out. Because you belong with him. With them. Just as you belong with Sophie and Jilly." The smile he gave her promised the whole world.

Chapter Twenty-One

The Landseer Motel, one hour later...

Jesse ushered his children out the door of Unit One while Farren followed him. "Thanks for letting us use the room to change, Farren."

"Thank you," his children chorused.

Tyler looked at the lifeguard stand. "But Eva's not up there. I can't go in the pool if she's not there."

"I'll be in the water with you, buddy."

"But I want her." A pout began to form. Before it could grow into an angry outburst, Jesse swung him to his shoulders.

"See? I'll take you into the pool like this."

Raine and Thea were already in the pool enclosure, delighted that they were here on a surprise day. They'd become accustomed to alternate weekends at the motel since Jesse had joined Singles' Fest.

"Raine! Thea!" Two shouts broke through the happy babble of voices around the pool.

Jesse looked toward the office and saw Eva, Sophie, and Jilly rushing across the lawn toward them. The girls ignored him and raced into the pool enclosure to greet his daughters excitedly. Eva, looking more beautiful than he'd ever seen her, followed at a more dignified pace, her eyes, locked with his, were wide and happy.

He blinked but the vision of her didn't waver, didn't disappear.

She was his and was striding with clear purpose.

He was about to be claimed.

His throat closed with emotion. He'd loved Lynne unconditionally, but they'd been young, and easy. They'd dated, fallen for each other, married happily with family support on both sides.

But this, with Eva, had been hard fought, painful, almost lost too many times to count. This new future would be all the sweeter because of the pain it took to get here.

His heart thudded and his breath matched each stride she took toward him.

"Eva!!" Tyler called her in a high-pitched scream painted by delight and surprise. He joggled and bounced in excitement. Soon, Tyler on his shoulders would be impossible. As it was, Jesse felt a sway that threatened a tumble. "You're here!!"

His son was speaking for him, too, because he couldn't find the words he needed. "Hi, Tyler," she said with a smile and a high five.

"I can go in the pool now, Daddy. Let me down."

"Okay."

His son trotted off and for a blessed moment, he had Eva alone. "Are you okay with this? I heard from Bernie, and I hoped we could have a family meeting." He cocked his eyebrow, hoping she'd catch the phrase family meeting, and it would mean to her what it meant to him.

"You wanted to ambush me, since that's what they did this morning." She laughed as she spoke and her eyes, her beautiful eyes, filled with love. His heart stopped, as he struggled to maintain his composure.

"Eva." He wanted to kiss her stupid, right here and now. He glanced over his shoulder to check out the kids in the pool. Tyler was trying to engage them in a splashing contest, but the girls were having none of it.

"Apparently it's a day for lots of changes," Eva said, claiming his attention again. She placed her hands on his biceps and held on. "Keeping this secret from the children any longer is unfair. I assume you feel the same?" She drew in a deep breath.

All he could manage was a nod, but his heart started again, so that was something.

"Everyone seems to agree, including the Morgans," she continued. "On the walk over here, I told Sophie and Jilly that I had a good friend who I met when I was lifeguarding for Singles' Fest. I said my friend had three children they could be friends with, too."

He nodded once more before saying, "I love you. And I want Sophie and Jilly in our lives as much as you do. I told Raine and Thea pretty much the same thing. They didn't appreciate hearing that my girlfriend had two daughters, but they'll figure things out pretty quick."

"I love you, too," she replied with a shy smile. "And I want Raine, Thea, and Tyler in our lives," she echoed.

He tilted his head. "And Sal and Tina?"

She nodded. "And Estelle and Bernie?"

"Yes."

"How do we make this happen?" Her lips widened into a smile that rivaled the sun dancing off the water in the pool. She made a huge circle with her arms. "It's big, this family we're proposing. Can it work?"

"It can if we try." He turned to watch the children in the pool. "Their grandparents want to be in their lives, we want each other and all our kids. And when it gets too much, we'll have free babysitting."

"Okay, I like the sound of that." She hesitated, looking lost. "How do we tell them about us?"

"Like this," Jesse said and gathered her into his arms. He kissed her right there in broad daylight, in front of their five goggling children at The Landseer Motel.

EVA FELT JESSE'S KISS down to her toes. His body felt hard, perfect against hers. They'd spent the night in each other's arms and had shown each other all the love they had to give.

And they had plenty.

Her morning hadn't gone as planned. Her day so far was better than she could dream. She drew back and then rested her head against

Jesse's shoulder. "I'll tell you more detail later, but Estelle is opening doors to me I believed were slammed shut."

"The fall made both Bernie and Estelle think hard about what would happen if one of them became ill or disabled. They're lucky all that happened was a severe sprain. It's a challenge for anyone to raise children and the older they get the busier they get. Bernie and Estelle are still vital and fit, but I'm glad they've looked ahead."

"Estelle's gone to grief counselling, too. She says it's helped a lot." Jesse's heart sounded steady and strong under her ear.

"We've got five children staring at us," he said, his voice a rumble in his chest. "Time to face the music."

They disengaged, clasped hands, and walked to the gate of the pool enclosure. "Want to talk about this?" She asked the children who stood in the pool, mouths agape at the scene they'd witnessed.

Raine nodded and swam to the steps to leave the pool. Her sister stayed behind, looking from her dad to Eva. A smile tilted her lips up and Eva responded with one in kind.

Then, when she realized Raine had taken the lead, Sophie joined her. The two oldest rose from the water, took a stab at drying off and came to stand on the pool side of the chain link fence.

"How long have you liked each other?" Raine asked.

"I came on a fishing weekend with Uncle Archie and met Eva then. After that, we saw each other a time or two as friends," he hedged. "But after a while, I came to see that I enjoyed being with her." He looked at Eva expectantly and she took her cue.

"I liked him, too, because of how nice and kind he is. Except I was worried about being a stepmom again when all I really wanted was to get my children back. You don't know this, Raine, but—."

Raine interrupted her. "We know that Sophie and Jilly weren't allowed to see you except for Wednesday's on your video chat. Sophie told us at the park."

"Oh. Sophie, you have no idea how sorry I am that it took this long to sort out everything. Grownups make mistakes, get stubborn and don't always look at different solutions for problems."

Sophie smiled. "It's okay, Mom, we knew things would work out sooner or later." She bit her lip and went on. "I couldn't talk about this stuff at school because the kids there already knew we lived with Gramma and Grampa. If I talked about you, they'd have more questions I couldn't answer. I'm glad I got to tell Raine and Thea about you. They understood because they don't have their mom, either."

Eva's heart contracted at her daughter needing to vent to another child about how the adults in charge had messed up. Children were resilient, but she ached that they needed to be. "Again, I'm sorry, Sophie. But life will be different now."

Raine smiled. "If we have to share our dad, we're glad it's with our best friends." She flung her arm across Sophie's shoulder. Sophie nodded.

Jesse shifted beside her, and Eva saw him thumb his eyes. "I don't know how you got to be this smart."

"Easy," his daughter said, "I'm like Mom. She was real smart about life."

"Yes, she was." His voice broke and Eva heard a suspicious sniff. Again, Jesse handled an emotional moment without hiding his reaction or turning away.

She was so blessed to have found him.

After their swim, the children played in the playground where Tyler scared the life out of Eva by hanging upside down for far too long. She wanted to grab him off the bar, but Jesse held her back saying boys liked pushing their limits and his boy was no different.

Realizing she had some things to learn about boys, she subsided, but kept a sharp eye on Tyler.

Jilly and Thea came over to see her. "Momma, will you come to the park to catch frogs with us?"

"I will if you want me to." She looked at Thea, who sweetly took her hand.

Thea smiled and nodded. "We want you to see the pond and everything," the child said through a long breath.

"Thank you. I'll come this week I promise."

Jilly nodded at Thea. "She always keeps her promises," she said solemnly.

Half an hour later, they decided to stroll the beach and head to the J Roger for fish and chips. She and Jesse held hands while the children ran ahead, looked for crabs and splashed in waves that swept the shoreline.

"This all seems normal and natural. And if I had to put a word to it, I'd say this last hour has been anti-climactic."

"Are you saying the drama was all in our heads?" Jessed tugged her close to his side, where she settled her arm around his waist.

"No, but now that it's behind us, I see nothing but clear skies ahead." Her heart was light, her thoughts clear.

As they neared the restaurant the children gathered around them, a small herd of happy, healthy children that she and Jesse would share. Eva blinked back tears and smiled up at him. "Are you as amazed as I am?"

"Boggled," he said. "But I haven't felt this happy in years. Since Tyler was born. Since before Lynne's diagnosis."

She squeezed his hand in response, knowing that whatever life threw at them, they could weather it together.

When he heard his name, Tyler piped up. "Smooching is okay between friends as long as they both want to."

"Is it okay that we want to?" she asked him.

"Yep!"

FIVE MONTHS LATER...moving day.

"This is the last of the boxes," Jesse said as he shouldered his way through the crowd of helpers. Eva, Tina, and Estelle had taken charge in the kitchen and worked together to fill cupboards and drawers with kitchen gear. Their soft, feminine voices came to him as he passed the kitchen on his way to the stairs. Estelle asked where Eva wanted the pots and pans and didn't raise a breath of objection when Eva told her where to put them.

Progress came in small steps, and he smiled to think how much easier life had become with each one.

Upstairs, Bernie and Sal busied themselves putting the children's bunkbed sets together. He heard a thud and a mild curse floated out of the room. Must be Bernie, who had a hit and miss relationship with hand tools. Mostly hit. But he had to hand it to the man, he never quit trying.

He headed down the hall for the main bedroom. The bedroom he'd share with his wife tonight. Double walk-in closets and a larger ensuite bath would give them more room. He'd been happy to surprise her with her comfy reading chair and favorite floor lamp tucked into the corner. He could see her settling in for some peace and quiet as she read her favorite mysteries. His taste ran to political thrillers, and he enjoyed trading them with Bernie. They were working on getting Sal hooked, too.

A household with five active children needed more room than his previous home and Rook's Nest Cottage combined. With *NanaBanana* up and running and Eva also running a babysitting agency for tourists, buying a larger home close to the school in Summerville made sense.

He'd assumed that each set of sisters might want to share their rooms, but he'd been wrong. The two older girls, Sophie and Raine, wanted to room together. Jilly and Thea agreed that they did, too. Not only were they stepsisters but best friends. Tyler lorded it over them all that he was the only one in the family who had his own room, including his parents.

He stepped into the room he considered a haven now that they'd returned from their too-brief honeymoon at The Sands. Eva hadn't wanted to go far from the children, so they'd hidden away in Last Chance Beach and done nothing but be together.

There was no better way to start their lives as husband and wife, partners, friends, allies.

Living near the school meant Sophie and Jilly could be with them alternate weeks. Bernie and Estelle were feeling their way through this time, but they'd mentioned the idea of extended travel to Europe. He saw a time coming when all their children lived under one roof most of the time. At last, Eva would have her family back together permanently.

When that time came, and the Morgans were comfortable with the idea, they'd proceed with adopting Sophie and Jilly. He'd already started on the path for Eva to adopt Raine, Thea, and Tyler.

Sal and Tina had accepted Eva easily. After the subterfuge and half-truths that had marked the early days of their relationship, he'd been relieved to have everything in the open.

Eva slipped into the bedroom behind him and closed the door. He heard a snick of the lock. "This is it? Everything's here now?" She indicated the box in his arms.

He nodded. "The last box containing winter clothes. We need to unpack it soon. The weather's changing." He tilted his head. "Aren't the kids coming home from school any minute?"

"Not yet," she murmured, and walked toward him, her eyes shining and her hips swaying. "Not this minute. This minute is for you and me."

"You and me," he agreed and took her into his arms. "Our kids can wait."

MAKE ME, the romance between Archie Jones and Beth Mathews will be available October 9, 2023, in print and ebook. Pre-orders are being taken now.

Archie and Beth inherit their shared nephews and niece as the result of a tragedy. Archie's never seen himself as dad material, but there's something about Beth that calls to him. His outrageous suggestion that they live together and raise the children as a family gives her the chance to plan a legal challenge for full custody, while Archie's planning a romantic campaign to win her heart. But first, he must quit lying about the threat to their joint custody agreement.

If you love forced proximity, fake relationships, and easy humor you'll enjoy **Make Me.**

IF YOU ENJOYED *Take Me (and My Kids)* and have ever found a wonderful romance by reading reviews, please pay it forward by sharing a few words about how *Take Me (and My Kids)* made you feel when you closed it. A review doesn't have to be long, or a retelling of the plot, just a few words on how you felt when you finished. Did you sigh at the end? Feel happy?

If you want to hear about exciting new releases and deals you can subscribe to Bonnie's Newsy Bits on my website. Readers can download a free short romance set in Last Chance Beach when they subscribe. All my romance titles are listed on my website at https://www.bonnieedwards.com/

Fake Me by Bonnie Edwards
How to fake out a meddlesome matchmaker - fake date the match!

International real estate broker Grady O'Hara, unkempt, miserable, and nursing his battered heart, is holed up in the Landseer Motel in Last Chance Beach. A first-class grump, Grady's appalled that enthusiastic sprite, Farren Parks wants him to open his motel to single parents looking for love.

He suspects his sister has sent Farren to lure him into a romance. Again. The last one ended in disaster.

Farren expects him to tolerate children laughing, splashing, and squealing. Big no! Crowds of happy families? Bigger no!

He does not want a second chance at life. Or love.

Unless Farren agrees to fake date him to fake out his meddlesome matchmaking sister...

Grady soon plays handyman, painter, and business advisor to Farren's fledgling business, Singles Fest. The happy sound of children in the pool doesn't grate on his nerves as he expected. He sees parents making romantic connections that stir his heart.

But an old flame of Farren's has arrived and Grady wakes up to another looming loss if Farren gives her first love a second chance. The rival has brought his adorable kids to the motel.

A rival who's clearly looking for a new wife...

DID YOU KNOW?

Last Chance Beach was created by a group of romance authors back in 2020. We wanted to have a summer place where the living was easy and the romance perfect! We're mid-series now with lots of books available and many more to come. You'll find sweet romances to steamy, a bit of suspense, blended families, there may even be a bit of spooky.

But most of all, you'll be swept away to our lovely seaside town where all the endings are happy. You can find the books already available here: https://www.amazon.com/dp/B09S3BGDZ including my title, **Fake Me.** Some books are also available at other retailers. Please check your favorite store.

You can also get updates and hang out with the authors and readers of the series in the exclusive Facebook Group **Last Chance Beach Romance Readers**.

Recent and Upcoming Last Chance Beach Titles

Fake Me – Aug 15/21 – Bonnie Edwards
Masquerade Under the Moon – Oct 2/22 – Kari Lemor
Island Treasure – Nov/22 - Susan R. Hughes
Where Dreams Come True – Dec/22 Judy Kentrus
Beating in Time - Feb/23 - MJ Schiller
You...Again – Mar/23 - Nancy Fraser
Take Vitamin Sea for Love – Jun/23 -Annee Jones
Solace Under the Stars - Jul/23 – Kari Lemor
Make Me – Oct/23 - Bonnie Edwards (available for pre-order)
Beacon of Thanks– Nov/23 – Judy Kentrus
And more in 2024!

Don't miss out!

Visit the website below and you can sign up to receive emails whenever Bonnie Edwards publishes a new book. There's no charge and no obligation.

https://books2read.com/r/B-A-JXD-HQKYB

BOOKS 2 READ

Connecting independent readers to independent writers.

Did you love *Take Me (and My Kids)*? Then you should read *Fake Me*[1] by Bonnie Edwards!

How to fake out a meddlesome matchmaker - fake date the match!

International real estate broker Grady O'Hara, unkempt, miserable, and nursing his battered heart, is holed up in the Landseer Motel in Last Chance Beach. A first-class grump, Grady's appalled that enthusiastic sprite, Farren Parks wants him to open his motel to single parents looking for love. He suspects his sister has sent Farren to lure him into a romance. Again. The last one ended in disaster.

Farren expects him to tolerate children laughing, splashing, and squealing. Big no! Crowds of happy families? Bigger no!

He does not want a second chance at life. Or love.

---

1. https://books2read.com/u/47O8La

2. https://books2read.com/u/47O8La

Unless Farren agrees to fake date him to fake out his meddlesome matchmaking sister...

Grady soon plays handyman, painter, and business advisor to Farren's fledgling business, Singles Fest. The happy sound of children in the pool doesn't grate on his nerves as he expected. He sees parents making romantic connections that stir his heart.

But an old flame of Farren's has arrived and Grady wakes up to another looming loss if Farren gives her first love a second chance. The rival has brought his adorable kids to the motel. A rival who's clearly looking for a new wife...

FAKE ME is a standalone novel in a new line of contemporary romances set in Last Chance Beach, written by bestselling and award-winning authors who deliver something for every romance lover.

About the Author

Bonnie Edwards has been published by Kensington Books, Harlequin Books, and Carina Press. With over 40 romance titles to her credit, she has been translated into several languages and sold books worldwide. Learn more at https://www.bonnieedwards.com/

www.ingramcontent.com/pod-product-compliance
Lightning Source LLC
Chambersburg PA
CBHW020431180626
46812CB00003B/1178